ROBYN DONALD

Indiscretions

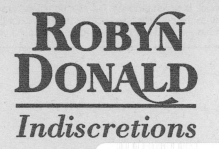

Harlequin Books

TORONTO • NEW YORK • LONDON
AMSTERDAM • PARIS • SYDNEY • HAMBURG
STOCKHOLM • ATHENS • TOKYO • MILAN
MADRID • WARSAW • BUDAPEST • AUCKLAND

ISBN 0-373-11794-9

INDISCRETIONS

First North American Publication 1996.

Copyright © 1995 Harlequin Books S.A.

Robyn Donald is acknowledged as author of this work.

Bride's Bay Resort

NEW ZEALAND/JAPANESE TRADE
DELEGATION

ITINERARY

INFORMAL PRELIMINARY EVENTS

Day 1
Inaugural dinner (private dining room)
Day 2
Morning
Golfing session
Afternoon
Rifle range
Evening
Dinner—New Zealand and Japanese
delegates meeting separately
Day 3
Fishing trip—delegation to meet at the
hotel marina.
Afternoon
Golfing session
Evening—free

TRADE TALKS

Day 4 and morning of day 5

GUEST REGISTER

Mr. Watanabe
Mr. McCabe
Peter Sanderson
Susan Waterhouse

Nicholas Leigh

Mariel Browning

Dear Reader,

When I was asked to write a book for the BRIDE'S BAY RESORT series I was flattered and aware that I should say no, as I don't write about places I've never been to. However, second thoughts prevailed. As my husband, Don, and I were going to be in North America that summer it was easy enough to add on a side trip to South Carolina.

We loved it. The hospitality was superb, the food magnificent and the scenery with its intricate blending of land and sea reminded me just a little of home. It was the first time I'd been to the South; I suspect I may have left a small corner of my heart there. I hope you enjoy *Indiscretions* as much as I enjoyed exploring this delightful area of America.

Yours sincerely,

Robyn Donald

ROBYN DONALD has always lived in Northland in New Zealand, initially on her father's stud farm at Warkworth, then in the Bay of Islands, an area of great natural beauty, where she lives today with her husband and an ebullient and mostly Labrador dog. She resigned her teaching position when she found she enjoyed writing romance novels more, and now spends any time not writing in reading, gardening, traveling and writing letters to keep up with her two adult children and her friends.

Books by Robyn Donald

CHAPTER ONE

"I THOUGHT YOU'D BE interested."

Wide blue eyes shaded with cynicism, Mariel Browning lifted her brows at the bartender. "Why?"

"Well, they *are* fellow countrymen of yours. You can't meet many of them—didn't you tell me there are only three million of you?"

"I did, but at least half of those are overseas at any one time."

She grinned at the look he sent her over the top of his spectacles. Desmond was too good a bartender to show any disbelief, but she'd met him several times over the past year and was beginning to be able to read his expressions. This one said, *Pull the other leg!*

"Well, that's the way it seems," she amended, her smile and tone edging into irony. "I trip over New Zealanders all the time. They're everywhere. When their kids grow up the first thing they want to do is fly away from those three little islands at the furthermost ends of the earth and see what the rest of the planet is like. In any group of more than five people anywhere in the world, you can be sure that one of them is a New Zealander." She smiled to soften the stiffness in her tone. "Yes, even here in South Carolina, where most people don't know New Zealand exists, and those few who do think it's part of Australia."

The middle-aged black man, who had been one of the latter, gave her a stately smile as he set the tall glass of gently fizzing mineral water in front of her. "But these are important New Zealanders," he said seriously.

"The Minister of Trade, no less, here to talk business with his Japanese counterpart. Big deal," she said lightly, hiding a tiny niggle of unease with a dazzling smile. Where there were politicians intent on conferring there would also be diplomats, discreetly powerful, unobtrusive and necessary.

Until her arrival on Jermain Island, one of the Sea Islands off the coast of South Carolina, she'd believed she was going to be interpreting for a group of businessmen. Noted for her fluency in Japanese and her ability to navigate flawlessly through the ideographs of its written language, Mariel always enjoyed coming to Bride's Bay Resort. However, had she been told this was a diplomatic occasion, she'd have looked for some excuse to stay away.

She had reason, she thought with a twist of her full mouth, to be wary of diplomats.

The cool mineral water slid down her throat as she looked appreciatively around Desmond's domain. Some forty years ago the bar had been planned to reflect the stately, country-house sophistication of an English gentleman's club. Mariel had never been in an English club, but she thought the designer had produced a very pleasant atmosphere.

But then, the hotel was noted for its beauty and refined ambience. That was one of the reasons it was so popular with high-powered groups of businessmen and diplomats for semiofficial meetings like the one ahead.

After a moment she said restlessly, "I don't know that I count as a Kiwi anymore—I've been away for the past ten years." Ever since she was eighteen.

And I didn't enjoy it much while I was there, she added silently. *Hated it, in fact.*

"You've still got an accent," Desmond said, looking past her as a man entered the room and sat at one of the tables.

Moving toward the newcomer, he said professionally, "Good afternoon, sir. What can I get for you?"

"Weak whiskey and soda, please."

In spite of herself, Mariel's head turned. Although the newcomer's deep textured voice invoked an involuntary feminine response, it was the accent that caught her attention most. Far from a conspicuously antipodean drawl, the unmistakable intonation and rhythm nevertheless proclaimed his antecedents.

Definitely one of the New Zealand party.

And a diplomat to boot.

Certainly not a politician. For a start, he was too young. Thirty-four at the outside, showing a smooth elegance that hinted of a lifetime accustomed to the confidence and privileges that only social position and money can buy.

Some of that money, Mariel decided, covertly evaluating him with an eye honed in embassies as a child, had been spent on an exclusive London tailor.

Not that his clothes made him. Oh, he certainly wore them well, his suit clinging lovingly to broad shoulders and long limbs, but there was much more to the man than excellent tailoring. Shocked, she registered a subtle tug at her senses, more antagonism than excitement, as her eyes lingered on the play of muscle when he stretched his legs and picked up a newspaper from the rack beside his chair.

And then, as if he'd known all along of her sideways scrutiny, he looked directly at her, all icy appraisal. It hit her like a blow. Mariel knew she was no raving beauty, but perhaps she had become too accustomed to the involuntary homage most men paid to red-brown hair and ivory skin and large blue eyes with enough turquoise in them to make them intriguing.

Not, however, this man, this New Zealander. The only emotion in his expression was an uncompromising assessment, calculating and studied, that flicked her self-esteem.

He thinks I'm trying to pick him up, she realized. The nerve of the man! What conceit!

Forgetting her normal caution, she allowed an amused, condescending curve to widen her soft lips. David had told her often that when she smiled like that, the tiny creases at the corners of her mouth deepened, giving her a smile of sultry aloofness that both beckoned and discouraged. For some reason she hoped David had been right. Coolly, with measured, leisurely deliberation, she looked the newcomer over from beneath dark lashes, keeping her eyes steady, almost placid.

He suffered her scrutiny with an impervious, bored self-assurance, his only measurable response being the slight narrowing of pale eyes that gave him the concentrated, vigilant stare of a hunter.

An atavistic fear shivered through Mariel, but pride kept her head high, kept that small, provoking smile pinned in place as she ran her gaze across the arrogant features of the newcomer's face. And it was pride that lifted her shoulders—although nobody would ever be able to say for sure that she'd shrugged as she turned away. Yet even as she presented her back to the newcomer, she felt the lash of his glance. Adrenaline surged through her, tightening her skin, hurrying her breath. *Fool,* her brain said. *Fool, fool, fool...*

It would have been more sensible to suffer that antagonistic glance passively, because beneath the newcomer's instant hostility she discerned another, equally potent response. In the first few seconds of that intent, wordless communication, senses older and more primitive than the five most obvious had homed in on his interest. And she was experienced enough in the battle between the sexes to understand that a dangerous combination of pique and reluctant interest had driven her to issue a challenge.

Sexual attraction was a wild card, ungovernable, a matter of dangerous chemistry. It could play the very devil with your life, which was why she refused to allow it any place in her emotions, let alone her career.

Yet that primal call of male to female had goaded her into flinging his barely concealed antipathy back in his face. And although he had immense mastery over his expression so that not a muscle moved, not an eyelash flickered, no color licked along the prominent cheekbones, he hadn't been able to hide his sharp, fierce reaction. She could smell it, she thought, forcing herself to lift her glass to her mouth, feel it like the crackle of electricity against suddenly sensitized skin.

And she brought it on herself, behaving like a cheap idiot in a singles bar. Over the years she had evolved rigid rules. She had just overturned one of the most important: *Never get involved with a client.*

So it was alarming that one glance from a total stranger should propel her over the invisible line of demarcation.

Even more alarming was the fact that every cell in her body was still caressed by a purring, lazily feminine satisfaction that had nothing to do with the normal rules of daily life and everything to do with the man who sat so silently a few yards away.

Desmond delivered his drink and came back to the bar. It was the slack time of day, when he ran the place by himself for an hour. Without being obvious he turned up the Mozart on the tape.

"Know him?" he asked softly.

A spot between her shoulder blades prickled. She shook her head. "Never seen him before," she said, easing her dry throat by swallowing half her drink.

"Well, he looks as if he finds that red hair and those long legs mighty interesting," Desmond said neutrally.

Resisting the impulse to lift her heavy, shoulder-length tresses clear of her neck, Mariel tilted her glass, keeping her eyes on the bubbles fizzing up through the clear liquid. "He's a guest," she muttered.

As well as clients, guests were out of bounds. And she had just stepped over those bounds. Still angry with herself—and the unknown man with the unsettling glance—she asked, "When does the rest of the diplomatic party arrive?"

Desmond knew everything about the hotel, including, rumor had it, the identity of the man who was the lover of Liz Jermain, the resort manager.

"They're meeting the launch at four o'clock," he told her, "so they'll be here in a couple of hours. The New Zealanders, that is. The Japanese arrive forty minutes later by helicopter."

Mariel had been at the hotel for no more than an hour herself, just time to unpack in the small room she'd been allocated in the staff quarters, put out the items that made each impersonal room a temporary home and order the flowers she always needed to sustain the illusion.

She drained her glass. "Thanks, Desmond. That saved my life."

"You should eat more," he said disapprovingly. "Languages are all very well, but they don't put meat on those thin bones. And you've got shadows under your eyes, too. I thought I told you last time—"

"Tell the people I work for," she said, smiling. "They're the ones who drag me out of bed to translate and interpret, and keep me working all night."

"But you like it."

"Wouldn't do anything else. See you later—I'd better go and talk to Elise."

He nodded, looking sober. "Poor girl," he said.

"Is her husband still giving her a hard time?"

Desmond frowned. "Something is," he said, exercising his famous discretion.

"I'd better go. See you later."

Still acutely conscious of the man who sat apparently intent on the newspaper, Mariel walked with brisk steps across the room. Intuition warned her that the stranger was aware of every footfall. *I hope he hates it as much as I do,* she thought, trying to smooth away the raw patch his instant contempt had left on her psyche.

She turned away from the foyer, its cool elegance warmed by great jardinieres filled with the flowering azaleas that were nature's tribute to spring. Ahead lay the hotel's business center, set up with the latest in equipment. Elise Jennings, who ran it and organized the staff necessary to deal with anything a diplomat, industrialist or business leader might need, had been going through a particularly difficult time. Her marriage had broken up messily, and she'd been forced to sell her home on the mainland and move into staff quarters with her seven-year-old daughter.

Normally a quiet, reserved person, Elise had wept on Mariel's shoulder the last time she'd been at Bride's Bay, and they'd talked for hours. This time, however, although the older woman looked just as tired and heartsick, she greeted Mariel with pleasure.

"Good to see you again. How's New York?"

"Noisy," Mariel said, adding delicately, "How's Caitlin?"

Elise frowned. "Just the same. Very dependent," she said briefly.

"Are you still living in the staff quarters?"

"Yeah, and she still wants to go to California to be with Jimmy. I can't convince her that she's better off here with me—she thinks she'd be able to go to Disneyland every day."

"Poor kid."

"I know." Looking down at the sheaf of papers in her hand, Elise said bitterly, "You remember I told you last time I thought he was up to something? Well, my noble Jimmy decided he wasn't going to share any of his hard-won assets, so he declared bankruptcy. Caitlin and I have nothing."

Appalled, Mariel asked, "Can he do that?"

The older woman gave her a cynical smile. "Honey, if you've got a good enough lawyer, you can do just about anything. Oh, I can understand it. He grew up on the island here—in a little house down by the fishing wharf—and he had nothing. It was sheer guts and working his butt off for years that got him where he is. He isn't about to share any of it. Well, he lost, too, because I've got custody, and there's no way I can afford to fly Caitlin and me out to California. And I'm not letting her go without me."

The telephone interrupted her. Elise picked it up and said, "Yes, sir, we can do that right away." When she'd replaced the receiver she said, "Mariel, you're needed in room 27. The guy wants a document translated from English to Japanese."

"I thought the New Zealand lot weren't coming until four," Mariel complained mildly, getting to her feet. "Oh, well, no rest for the wicked." With her luck it would be the antagonistic stranger in the bar who wanted her.

"An eager beaver," Elise said. "Learned any new languages lately?"

Mariel grinned. "Basque. It's supposed to be the most difficult language in the world."

"Is it used much?"

"Almost never." Mariel met her surprised gaze with a slow twinkle. "Only six hundred thousand or so people speak it."

"Then why learn it?"

"The challenge," Mariel said cheerfully as she turned to go. "I can't resist a challenge."

"Hey, how much do you know?"

"I can say 'good morning' and 'good evening,' and I think I might have a handle on 'goodbye.' Beyond that it's a mystery."

She left the room to laughter and went swiftly up the gracious sweeping staircase, trailing her fingers over the elegant curves of the banister, worn smooth by thousands of hands over the years. There was nothing in New Zealand to match this, she thought with enormous contentment. Nothing at all.

The Sea Islands had waxed rich for generations, first on indigo, then on cotton, and always on the efforts of slaves. This glorious building was the original Jermain plantation house, its white pillars like an evocation of the Old South. After the Civil War the family and the plantation had fallen on hard times, until Liz Jermain's grandmother scraped up the money to join the two flanking buildings to the main house and transform it into a hotel.

Outside room 27 Mariel took a deep breath and straightened her shoulders before knocking. The door opened immediately, and yes, it was the man from the bar.

His eyes, so pale a green they were almost colorless—except for glints of gold blazing through a matrix of jade—held hers for a moment before the professional politeness in his expression changed to cold aloofness. But he couldn't prevent a flicker of elemental response.

Shockingly, an inchoate flutter of anticipation in Mariel's stomach burned suddenly into excitement.

"Good afternoon," she said, her formal smile hiding a perilously balanced composure. "You want a document translated, I believe."

His lashes half covered his eyes, intensifying that disturbing glitter. "Yes, from English to Japanese. Can you do it?"

"Certainly, sir."

"Here," he said curtly, "in this room."

She did not want to sit at the charming desk beside the magnificent four-poster bed and work while he watched her, and she certainly didn't care for his implied mistrust. Without thinking, she shook her head. "I use a computer...."

"A portable, surely?"

Lord, but her wits had gone begging. "Yes," she said woodenly. "But—"

"This is confidential, Ms. . ."

The keen eyes had missed nothing, certainly not the absence of rings on her long slender fingers. "Browning," she said stiffly.

"How do you do, Ms. Browning. My name is Nicholas Lee."

Automatically she took the hand he held out. Although his grip was firm it wasn't painful, but an instant sizzle of electricity made her draw a sharp breath into her lungs. Without thinking, she jerked her hand away.

Damn, the man was dynamite, and he had to know it.

However, nothing of that recognition showed in the hard, handsome face nor in the green-gold eyes, although some foolish, hidden part of her preened at the quick tightening of his mouth and the way his eyes narrowed even further, giving him a hooded, menacing look.

He said smoothly, "I'm afraid I must insist that you work here, Ms. Browning." He added with an undertone of mockery that whipped across her confidence, "If you wish, I can leave the door open."

Color heated the soft ivory of her skin. He saw too much. "That won't be necessary, sir," she said, striving for the right touch of amusement, the note of casual sophistication that would put him in his place. "I'll get my computer."

"You understand that I'll expect you to translate into Japanese symbols?"

"My computer is quite capable of doing that, and so, Mr. Lee, am I," she said in what she hoped was a repressive tone.

When she'd arrived back he handed her a letter from a Japanese businessman, one of the country's most forward-looking industrialists.

"This is the letter I've answered," he said. "You might find it helpful to read it first so that you know what I'm talking about."

Apparently he had an interest in some new invention. Well versed as she was in the subtleties of Japanese business language, she realized that the industrialist had written to him as an equal.

So he had power.

Well, she didn't need a letter to tell her that. He reeked of it, she thought snidely; power and the personality to make use of it oozed from every pore of his tall, graceful body.

Doing her best to ignore his potent male presence, she got to work. His name, she realized, looking at the slashing black signature, wasn't Lee; it was Leigh.

It figured. She wasn't surprised that his name should have the more complex spelling; *he* was complex. Not to mention prejudiced, she thought with irritation. He didn't know her, and yet he had presumed to judge her, and that before she'd been stupid enough to issue her own version of a sexual challenge.

Perhaps he had something against tall redheads who drank mineral water in bars.

Fortunately, because he was having an unsettling effect on her nerves, she had long ago perfected the skill of complete concentration. She needed it now. He'd given her a fairly complicated document which took some time to translate, but eventually she was able to say, "Here you are, sir, it's finished," and lay the three sheets down on the gleaming desk.

Clearly he shared her gift of losing herself in work, because she had to speak twice before he looked up from the sheaf of papers he was studying, black brows knotting as those disturbing eyes focused on her face.

"Read it to me, please. In Japanese."

Too well trained to ask why, she obeyed, her voice slipping through the liquid syllables with confidence.

"You have an excellent accent," he observed when she'd finished. "You must have learned to speak the language as a child."

Mariel returned impersonally, "Yes, sir."

"I see," he said, a dry note infusing his voice.

She asked, "When did you learn?"

And could have kicked herself. Normally she'd have stopped at a simple thank-you; natural caution should have overridden an unsuspected desire to learn more about him.

Although his brows drew together above the blade of his nose, he said mildly enough, "In my teens. I can speak the language fluently, and to a certain extent read it, but I can't write it and I'll never lose my accent."

Shrewdly Mariel surmised that this would always be a source of irritation to him. He would demand perfection from himself, as well as others—the very worst sort of man, totally impossible to live with.

She wasn't going to have to live with him. However, she was going to have to work with him, and that meant that from now on she was going to be resolutely, professionally, implacably aloof.

With a touch of brusqueness he resumed speaking. "Thank you, you've done a good job. I'll order tea. I assume you are a tea drinker? Most New Zealanders are, especially at this time of the afternoon."

No, he didn't miss anything. As well as keen eyes, he had keen ears. Although her American colleagues invariably picked up the trace of an antipodean accent in her speech, any New Zealanders she'd met during the past few years usually assumed she was American.

Mariel looked at her watch. "I'm sorry, sir," she said without expression, "but I need to be free when the other members of the delegation arrive." She gave him a businesslike smile, carefully not quite meeting his eyes, and as she got to her feet said in the same collected tone, "It was kind of you to think of it. Thank you."

He waited until she had packed up her computer and printer and was halfway to the door before saying, "I am not kind, Ms. Browning. I do, however, appreciate efficiency and intelligence."

Delivered in a cool, inflexible tone, the words sounded almost like a warning.

MARIEL SAW Nicholas Leigh again that night at the inaugural dinner. According to Liz Jermain, the purpose of the conference was to conduct a high-level but informal discussion of trade patterns.

Known worldwide for its exclusivity and superb service, the resort, with its health club and golf course and rifle range, its banquet rooms and world-class restaurant, its proud history of discretion and opulence, was the perfect place for such occasions.

However, in spite of the official lack of ceremony, someone had decided that these proceedings should begin with a dinner. Although both parties had brought their own interpreters, Mariel, clad in a black dress so circumspect it almost rendered her invisible, presented herself at the small lounge off the reserved dining room to mingle and make herself useful, which she did, stepping in when conversations stuttered and died, acting as a sort of subsidiary hostess, smoothing the diplomatic pathways.

Apart from a middle-aged woman with shrewd, worldly eyes and two extremely elegant women of about Mariel's age—all New Zealanders—the room was filled with the dark elegance of about twenty men in good-quality evening clothes. Most were comparatively young; only a couple were the same age as her parents would have been had they still been alive.

Deep inside her, a barely discernible foreboding faded to quiescence.

As always she eschewed alcohol; this time she chose club soda and lime. While she was thanking the waiter for mak-

ing a special trip to get it, she looked up to see Nicholas
Leigh talking to one of the younger women, a very attractive person with smoothly coiffed hair the color of newly
minted copper. The woman's fine, patrician features were
lit by a composed, gracious smile, but there was nothing
composed about the swift glance she sent him from beneath her lashes.

Dumbfounded as a hitherto cloaked emotion flared
abruptly and painfully into life, Mariel thought, *I'm jealous!*

And the vivid sexual awareness that had sprung so unexpectedly to life in the bar a few hours earlier began to assume a much more sinister aspect.

Sharply she turned her head away, glad when her glance
fell on a middle-aged Japanese man smiling at a younger
New Zealander, who looked to be at a loss. She set her jaw
and made her way toward them.

The older man was too sophisticated to reveal any sign of
relief when she joined them and introduced herself with a
deprecating remark, but the younger man greeted her with
a frown. He turned out to be Peter Sanderson, a career diplomat. Short and blocky, his expression pugnaciously intense, he had narrow, suspicious eyes that flicked hastily
from person to person as though he was terrified of missing something. However, after the first irritated glare at
Mariel, his brows straightened, and he smiled at her with
overbold interest.

She didn't like him, she thought when he asked her where
she was from.

"New York? You don't sound like a native of the Big
Apple," he said, watching her as though he suspected her of
lying.

She smiled. "I'm a New Zealander, Mr. Sanderson."

"But you're not one of our party," he said, his brows
meeting.

"I'm an interpreter and translater," she told him, smiling to take away the edge in her voice.

The older man interposed politely, "With an excellent grasp of Japanese."

Transferring the smile to him, she bowed. "You honor me too much."

After waiting impatiently for the formalities to be over, Peter Sanderson asked, "How long have you been living in America?"

Trying to hide the wariness in her voice, she told him. He continued asking questions, cloaking them with a veneer of politeness too thin to hide his determination to get answers. His tenacity made Mariel uneasy; she didn't like the way he watched her, as though assessing her value as a pawn to be played in some game she didn't understand.

She suspected that his attitude wasn't personal—he was probably the sort of person who valued people only for their use to him—but she had to struggle to maintain her aplomb.

Five minutes later she felt someone behind her and turned, her eyes meeting with a small shock those of Nicholas Leigh. The redhead was still with him, and for a moment a purely feminine challenge crystallized in the woman's pale gray eyes as they met Mariel's.

Nicholas made the introductions; the woman was Susan Waterhouse, an aide to the New Zealand minister of trade. Perfectly pleasant and charming, she was nevertheless blanketed by an aura of detachment—neither aloof nor indifferent, yet oddly uninvolved—except when she looked at Nicholas.

In spite of its resemblance to a social occasion, this event was business; Mariel was merely a necessary adjunct, like a computer or a printer. In fact, her profession meant that she should try to be as inconspicuous as possible. Yet she couldn't repress a spurt of indignation when Susan Waterhouse's eyes rested for sizzling seconds on Nicholas's arrogant, hard-edged countenance.

Distastefully ignoring the scuttling, furtive envy that crawled across her heart, Mariel looked away. The unaccustomed strength of her reaction added to her troubled apprehension. Within a few minutes she made her excuses and left them.

As with most diplomatic affairs the evening was run with slightly soulless efficiency. Exactly enough time had been allocated for two drinks, so just as Mariel finished her second glass, a concerted movement propelled her toward the dining room.

She sat in an alcove to one side of the main table, waiting in case she was needed and trying unsuccessfully to keep her gaze firmly directed away from where Nicholas Leigh sat, charcoal hair warmed with a sheen of bronze by the lights, the poised head held confidently high, features sculpted in angles and planes that were at once fiercely attractive and invulnerable.

Handsome didn't describe him exactly, she thought, catching him as he smiled at the middle-aged woman beside him. Handsome was too effete, too ordinary. He had the disciplined, inborn grace of a predator—judging by the letter she'd translated that afternoon, a very intelligent, clear-minded predator. His classical good looks, based on coloring and bone structure, were overshadowed by an effortless, supremely well-controlled strength and authority.

Just what was his position in this high-powered group of politicians and diplomats?

He sat at the main table, which meant he had influence.

Surely too much power and influence for a man of his age?

The skin along her cheekbones tingled. Steadfastly she kept her eyes on the two ministers at the center of the table, but as plainly as if she was staring at him she knew that Nicholas Leigh was looking at her. And even from that distance the impact of his elemental magnetism flared through her, heating her skin and churning her stomach and melting the vulnerable base of her backbone.

At last the head of the Japanese mission rose; his interpreter, a slim, bespectacled man, stood to one side. Mariel settled herself to listen intently and professionally.

He was good, but the New Zealand interpreter who followed was not. Technically, she thought objectively, he had the words, but he was missing the nuances. Once she exchanged a glance with the Japanese interpreter, a split-second communication in which neither face moved a muscle, but both understood perfectly.

When she looked away her gaze was captured and held by Nicholas Leigh's half-closed eyes. Carefully she gave him a small, meaningless smile and returned her attention to the speaker, but that hard, searching, far-too-perceptive glance set her heart thudding disconcertingly against her ribs.

At eleven o'clock the dinner broke up to mutual expressions of immense esteem. Mariel waited until everyone had gone before sliding out of her chair. One of the least enjoyable aspects of occasions such as this was watching others eat delicious meals, but because she never knew when she'd be called on, she preferred to eat offstage, so to speak. The sandwich she'd eaten before coming down had been enough to satisfy her, but she could, she thought with anticipation, enjoy a good cup of tea right then.

The door of the dining room closed behind her; she relaxed and had begun to head off for the staff cafeteria when a voice from behind said, "Ms. Browning."

Not *now*, she thought, forcing her features into a mask of composure before turning. "Mr. Leigh?"

"I'd like to buy you a drink, if I may."

This was definitely not a part of her job description. Sedately she responded, "I'm afraid I'm not encouraged to socialize with guests, sir."

A spark of temper lit his eyes to pure, flaming gold, but was instantly curbed. "I need your professional opinion, and I need it tonight.'' When she still hesitated he said levelly, ''We can do it like this, or I can insist on a formal meeting.''

He didn't raise his voice; he didn't have to. An implacable note in the even tones made itself more than obvious. Involuntarily Mariel looked across the foyer to where Mr. McCabe, the New Zealand trade minister, was standing with a small group of men. As if summoned, he glanced their way, his shrewd eyes going from her face to Nicholas's. The minister's gaze returned to her countenance, and he nodded with an air of authority.

''Very well,'' she said, surprising herself with her acquiescence, and in case he got the wrong impression, added a fraction of a second too late, ''sir.''

Heavy lids hooded his eyes. He said quietly, ''Thank you, Ms. Browning.''

CHAPTER TWO

HE TOOK HER to Desmond's bar, seated her in one of the wing chairs and ordered the mineral water she asked for, deciding on another weak whiskey and soda for himself.

While the waitress went off to get the drinks, he asked unexpectedly, "What's your first name?"

She bristled, but told him in a level voice.

Black brows climbed. "Where does it come from?"

"It's a derivative of Mary," she said. "A family name. My m-mother used to say it came from a princess a long way back in the family tree who was born in what is now Bavaria. Apparently she was a bit of a handful, so her long-suffering family married her off to a Viking. Eventually some of their descendants took the name with them to England."

"I'm almost certain Mariel is a place in Cuba. I wondered whether it had sentimental associations for your parents," he said blandly, "but it's unlikely any Westerners would have been there when you were conceived."

Her heart slammed to a halt. Before she could stop herself she shot a glance at him, her pulse kicking into overdrive when she met the elongated slivers of pure light that were his eyes.

"Yes," she said huskily, trying not to swallow.

Broad shoulders lifted in a shrug, but she knew he'd noticed her response. However, his voice was almost indolent, as he said, "You're the right build and height to be of German descent. Although your coloring looks more Norse."

Of course he wasn't so crude as to scrutinize her tall, long-limbed body. Nevertheless, although his dark lashes hid his eyes, she felt exposed to the naked force of his interest, and to her horror her skin pulled tight and an unfamiliar sensation prickled in her breasts. Appalled, she wondered how the mere sound of a man's—a stranger's—voice could produce such a violent and unwanted physical response.

"It was," she returned dismissively, "just a family story, and almost certainly untrue. Families get the weirdest ideas about their antecedents."

"Ah, all those ancestors who were supposed to be descendants of kings and turn out to have worked as swineherds on the royal estates," he said, a note of irony coloring the deep voice. "It's a natural human instinct, I suppose, to put the best gloss on one's circumstances."

Once more her eyelids flew up. She met a gaze that was cool and glinting, a face that was a subtle challenge. *He must know,* she thought dazedly.

No, he couldn't!

Dry-mouthed, she grabbed for equanimity. "I suppose it is. What did you want to talk to me about, Mr. Leigh?"

He waited until the waitress had departed, then said, "What is wrong with the New Zealand interpreter? And please call me Nicholas, as I fully intend to call you Mariel from now on."

She drank some mineral water, grateful for its cold fizz and soothing passage down her raw throat. "What made you think there was something wrong?" she countered, unsure of the correct way to deal with this.

"Your face and my own instinct. If I hadn't been sure of it, that swift glance you exchanged with your Japanese counterpart would have convinced me."

Dismayed, she said, "You can't have seen anything in my expression!"

"Don't worry, I'm sure no one else did. As I said, I happened to be wondering already, and your face was too still.

You looked as though you were urging him on, mentally helping him."

She blinked. This man was dangerously observant, and astute enough to understand what those keen eyes saw. Choosing her words with caution, she said, "There's nothing wrong with his work. He's a perfectly competent—"

"At this level," he interrupted ruthlessly, "competence is not good enough, as you are well aware."

Of course she was.

"Very well," she said steadily. "He's missing nuances."

"Right. I'll tell the minister."

That inconvenient curiosity drove her to ask, "Where do you fit into this?"

His wide, sensuously molded mouth moved in a smile that curled her toes. "I'm a diplomat," he said, the words almost a taunt.

"Your letter didn't sound as though—" She stopped and drew in a startled breath. God, how could she have said that? But he didn't seem like the diplomats she'd known. He stood out, elemental and untamed as a wolf amongst well-fed, domesticated lapdogs. She began again. "I thought you were a businessman."

His lashes were long and thick and dark, darker even than hers. They drooped for a second, then rose to reveal a cool, unreadable stare. "I have an interest—purely advisory—in a trust that deals with venture capital for ideas, some of which are exported."

She met the challenge of his glance with a glinting, blue-eyed one of her own. "What will happen to the interpreter? Will he be sacked?"

Unhurriedly he drank some of the whiskey, his expression guarded but assured. In his dinner jacket he was the epitome of elegance, perfectly at home in this luxurious place. "I doubt it very much," he said with an indifference that came close to being insulting. "He'll just get extra training. However, that's not the point. This is an important meeting, and we need the best. You can take his place."

"No!" The word was out before she was able to stop it.

"Why not?" he asked, that concentrated gaze speculative as he studied her face.

Resisting the compulsion of those gleaming eyes, she parried, "How do you know I'm any better?"

"Just before I came down to dinner I got a fax from Tokyo congratulating me on getting a Japanese secretary," he said dryly. "That's good enough for me."

Any further objection would have been suspicious; it might even give rise to questions. And although eight years ago when she'd done her first job for the hotel the security check had turned up nothing, she wasn't perfectly safe. She never would be. She knew, none better, that every new person who checked it could turn up a small piece of information that would, if followed through, eventually damn her.

But she said feebly, "I'm hired by the hotel."

His hard, beautifully chiseled mouth curved into a mirthless smile. "Somebody will contact the hotel management," he said smoothly.

Neither Liz Jermain, the manager, nor her formidable grandmother would refuse his request. The hotel's reputation had been built on just such extra services. And that, she told herself sternly, was what she was there for, after all—to make sure that everything went perfectly.

"Well, I was hired as a backup, so it will be all right," she said, trying not to sound as reluctant as she felt. "I was a bit worried about the other guy. He's good, but just not quite good enough. I wouldn't like anything I did to lose him his job." She stole a sideways glance, wondering whether she had appeased the curiosity her first instinctive refusal must have aroused.

It was impossible to tell. Although he smiled, no warmth reached his eyes, and there was an air of calculation about him that chilled her.

"Nothing you did would lose him his job," he said enigmatically. "If that happens—and it seems highly unlikely because good Japanese interpreters are fairly thin on the ground in New Zealand—it will be his own inadequacy that does it. So forget about him and think of this as your patriotic duty."

Did he see the tiny, momentary flicker of pain in her eyes, the sharp, deep inner reaction to his words? "What did Edith Cavell say just before she was shot? 'Patriotism is not enough.' I prefer to think I owe my loyalty to humanity."

"Naturally. However, it's almost impossible to grow up without feeling some sort of emotion for the country one was born in. Especially one as beautiful as New Zealand. How old were you when you left?"

"Eighteen."

"And where did you go then?"

"To Japan to teach English for a year."

He gave her another of those assessing glances. "That's a long way from home and a totally different culture. Were you homesick?"

"Not really," she said cautiously. "I was lonely, though, for a while."

"You were an adventurous eighteen-year-old."

"No more so than most." She stopped. "You can't be interested in this."

His smile had a spark of self-derision in it. "Oh, I'm always interested in a beautiful woman."

"Then you're lucky, because there are several in this room who seem more than interested in you," she said calmly, picking up her bag as she rose to her feet. She'd been conscious of those looks, some surreptitious, more quite open, since she'd been in the bar. For some reason they set her teeth on edge. It must have been this that added the sting to her tone as she went on, "Each one is much more beautiful than I am, I assure you."

"Sit down." He didn't touch her, didn't even move, but for a moment the breath stopped in her throat. "That was crass," he said stiffly. "I'm sorry."

He even looked sincere. Why, then, was she almost certain that he was lying, that his remark had been made intentionally?

It was impossible to imagine him being so insensitive unless he did it deliberately. Behind the spectacular face was a cold, incisive brain, and for some reason he was trying her out.

"Let's start again," he said. "What happened after your stay in Japan?"

She could walk away. It would be immensely satisfying, but it would be overreacting, and it would be stupid. Whoever Nicholas Leigh was, he was a guest.

And the resort paid her extremely good money to give the guests what they wanted. If he'd been rude or suggestive, Liz would have been the first to expect her to leave, but he hadn't.

Silently acquiescing, Mariel resumed her seat and gave herself time to calm down by picking up her drink and sipping it. She was being too sensitive, foolishly so.

"I joined a hotel chain as a management trainee," she said. "But when they discovered I had a talent for learning languages, they decided I should be an interpreter."

"Do you do a lot of traveling?" he asked.

Her shoulders moved slightly. "Yes, although not as much now as I used to."

"Where else have you been?"

"Oh, I had a wonderful six months in Paris honing my French accent, then I spent a couple of years in a Beijing hotel. I've been in Malaysia and Russia and Germany, but I'm based in America now."

"A well-traveled woman," he observed dryly, his eyes resting on her mouth for a heart-stopping second before flicking up to capture her gaze. "Where do you live?"

"In New York."

"Why there? I'd have thought Washington was a lot closer, and there'd be more call for your services there surely."

Lacking the rude intrusion of Peter Sanderson's earlier catechism, he sounded no more idly interested, yet she was sure he was by far the more dangerous of the two.

"I like New York," she said defensively. "And I deal mostly with business matters, not the diplomatic service." Impelled by the need to stop this inquisition, she said, "Where do you live?"

"In London at the moment. Why are you wearing a color that doesn't suit you?"

Startled, she flashed him an indignant look. "I'm paid to fade into the wallpaper," she said, then wondered whether perhaps she shouldn't have admitted her reasons for dressing badly.

Somehow it seemed to give him an advantage she sensed he wouldn't hesitate to exploit.

"So you wear clothes that make that glorious ivory skin sallow and drain those astonishing teal blue eyes and red-brown hair of color."

Although his tone was detached, almost indifferent, she detected strong emotions smoldering beneath his elegant, sophisticated exterior. She fought down a keen curiosity, a fierce, consuming awareness that fretted her nerve ends and eroded her hard-won self-sufficiency.

That, of course, was what had caused her first instinctive reaction when he'd suggested she interpret for the New Zealand party. She'd been afraid that if she became more intimately involved with the delegation, she would see too much of him for her peace of mind.

That was what she was still afraid of. The last thing she wanted was to get tangled up with Nicholas Leigh, who was all man and too clever by half.

And a diplomat.

Mutinously she kept silent, relaxing by force of will the hands that gripped her bag.

His glance lingered on the white knuckles as he asked casually, apparently giving up on the previous subject, "So what part of New Zealand did you grow up in?"

"A small town," she said evenly, trying not to sound evasive, adding, when it was obvious he wasn't satisfied, "in the King Country."

"You have family there still?"

"No. My family are all dead."

"I'm sorry." Oddly enough he sounded it.

She shrugged. "I'm sorry, too, but it happened a long time ago."

"So you are entirely alone?" His tone made it a question.

The temptation to invent a lover was almost irresistible, but the hard-won knowledge, gained over the years, that the fewer lies she told the less likely she was to be caught out, stopped such a panicky decision. "Yes," she said remotely.

He didn't pursue it. "Do you enjoy your job?"

"Very much. I've met some fascinating people, I work in very luxurious surroundings, and I get paid well."

"You don't look like a cat," he said, smiling as she stared at him. It was a subtle smile, complex and enigmatic, and she didn't know how to deal with it, especially when he went on, "Oh, you move well, but your body is more athletic than sinuous, and the faint hint of intransigence about you is not the smug, slightly taunting feline variety—it appears to be the result of your Viking ancestry."

"So why a cat?" she asked steadily.

His eyes, his face, his voice, issued a challenge. "Because you sound like one. That's what a cat asks—comfort, a few novelties to tease the brain, and security. And I doubt if a cat cares who provides for its wants."

It was an oddly intimate conversation, and he was frighteningly perceptive. Mariel smiled ironically as she raised her brows. "My looks must be deceiving," she said lightly. "I don't think I'm in the least intransigent—"

"I'm glad to hear it," he interrupted, mocking her.

She'd had enough. Any desire for a cup of tea had long since departed, and she ached with the deep, languid weariness of exhaustion.

"I'm tired, I'm afraid," she said, smiling, her eyes and face as candid as she could make them. "If you don't mind, I'll leave you now. Stay and finish your drink," she concluded as he rose with automatic courtesy. Hastily she leapt to her feet—too hastily, for she swayed slightly and must have lost color.

Instantly he was beside her, his hand a hard support against her back. "Are you all right?" he demanded.

No, she was not; her head was spinning, and she wished she could blame lack of food. Biting her lip, she drew away as quickly as she could, her nostrils flaring at the faint, barely discernible scent of him, an insidious, inciting mix of musk and salt.

"I'm fine," she said steadily. "Just tired."

He made a swift sound of irritation. "You haven't had dinner, have you?"

"I had a substantial snack before drinks. I'm not in the least hungry," she told him, hoping that her words convinced him. If anyone presented her with food she might well throw up, because her stomach was churning with something that definitely wasn't hunger.

His expression unreadable, he looked keenly into her face. "I'm sorry," he said. "That was totally inconsiderate of me. I'll order you a bar meal."

Something of her revulsion must have shown in her face, for before she could answer he said autocratically, "Then I'll see you to your room."

She shook her head. "I sleep in the staff quarters, a hundred yards or so away."

"I'll see you there."

"Mr. Leigh—Nicholas—there is no need. The security here is watertight."

"My mother," he explained calmly, "would never forgive me. She had few rules, but those she had were cast in iron and drummed into me as a child. One of them was that when you've bought a drink for a woman you see her to her door. And you should know by now that security is never watertight."

Mariel cast him a wary, exasperated glance. Although he was smiling there was a determination in his expression that told her it was no use; this man would do what he wanted regardless of how she felt.

"Very well then," she said coldly, walking out before him.

The staff who lived on-site were housed in the old stables, which had been converted into a neat complex behind the main hotel. At the end of a wide pathway that curled away beneath magnolia and live oak, the old brick building was sheltered behind a low wall. Between the hotel and staff quarters was a formal garden, where beds of azaleas bloomed beneath the still flowerless branches of crepe myrtles. It was April and, while winter had barely loosened its grip on New York, here the night air was cool, but the days were warm and getting warmer.

"A pretty setting," Nicholas said, looking around.

Pretty? Compared to some of the quarters Mariel had slept in, the compound was palatial! "The owner's husband is a keen gardener," she said quietly.

Perhaps Nicholas Leigh was right; perhaps she did like her creature comforts too much. Surely anyone who'd been brought up in comparative luxury, then faced at the age of eight with a sudden descent into poverty and austerity, could be excused for enjoying such beautiful surroundings.

The gentle hush of waves on the beach backgrounded Nicholas Leigh's voice as he said, "This reminds me a little of Auckland. The same scent—salt and flowers and green growing things."

"And humidity?"

"You don't like the Auckland climate?"

She shrugged. "I've never lived there."

"And you never want to." He let that sink in before asking, "Is it just Auckland you dislike or New Zealand as a whole?"

The words were delivered mildly, but she felt the taunt as clearly as though he'd snarled at her. "There's nothing for me there now," she said dismissively, glad they had reached a door of the middle block. "This is as far as you are allowed, I'm afraid," she said, and held out her hand.

"I'll see you tomorrow," he said, smiling narrowly.

She shivered, wincing at the spark of electricity that flashed between them again, fierce and fathomless. It took willpower to retrieve her hand without jerking it from his.

"It's a damned nuisance, isn't it?" he said almost conversationally. "However, I'm sure we're both strong-minded enough to resist it."

She stared at him.

"Don't pretend you don't know what it is." An oblique smile barely disturbed the corners of his mouth. "You felt it the moment I did."

"I did not!" And then, because her indignant response had given her away, she said angrily, "Look, I'm not interested—"

"You challenged me," he said with a forbidding curtness, "and you knew you were doing it. I could be tempted to take you up on it, but I don't think it would be sensible."

There was contempt in his voice, contempt, she realized, directed not only at her. Nicholas Leigh saw this attraction as a weakness and despised himself for it.

Wordlessly she turned, her emotions perilously close to the surface, and slipped through the door, closing it behind her. His frankness had shocked her, and yet a dangerously capricious part of her heart thrilled, because he, too, had no defense against the overwhelming intensity of that physical reaction.

Damn, she thought, Nicholas Leigh was turning out to be a real threat to her peace of mind. Fortunately she was only here for four days.

Nothing could happen in four days.

As she took out her room key, Elise hurried past. "Have you seen Caitlin?" she demanded.

Mariel brought her head up sharply. There had been a real note of fear in the woman's voice. "No. Why?"

"Oh, God. I've looked and looked and looked for her, but she's not here. One of the housemaids said she saw her hanging around outside. I think she might have run away."

"Run away?"

Elise drew in a deep breath and calmed down. "To her father. I'll have to go and look for her."

"Just wait a moment while I change my shoes and I'll come and help."

Mariel came back outside in time to hear Elise say in carefully controlled tones, "Yes, honey, I know you don't like living here much, but we have to stay here for a while."

Caitlin's voice, the whine not entirely hiding her real unhappiness, floated on the humid air. "If you let my daddy come back, we could live in our old house."

"Oh, darling, we can't ever go back."

"We can go and live with him!" Caitlin shouted. "He said so. I heard him. I don't want to live here, I want to go to California to live with Daddy."

Mariel hesitated, then, her heart aching for them both, went into her room. Poor Elise was going to have to deal with this herself.

BY THE TIME she arrived at the main building the next morning, the New Zealand interpreter had been shipped out. Mariel was told by Liz Jermain that she was to do whatever was required of her.

After stashing her computer in the business center, she walked briskly along to the room that had been set aside for the delegation to breakfast in, and suffered with as much composure as she could the introductions Nicholas Leigh made. Mr. McCabe, the trade minister, received her with professional affability, and the aides and various other underlings accepted her presence without much comment. Susan Waterhouse gave her a cool nod. Peter Sanderson watched her with an avidity she found both irritating and upsetting.

The morning, she discovered as Nicholas handed her a cup of coffee, was to be spent on the golf course, and as the Japanese interpreter was busy with documents she was on duty.

Nicholas was also a member of the golfing group. He played well, she decided acidly, keeping her eyes away from the controlled line of shoulder and thigh, the smooth skill and grace with which he swung. He certainly had excellent rapport with the Japanese trade minister and his aides, one of whom asked Mariel if she played.

"I'm afraid not," she said, meeting Nicholas's eyes without a blink. She most emphatically did not want to display her mediocre golfing skills in such company.

"A pity," the man said, smiling.

From then on she took care to stay as far out of the way as she could. She didn't need the attention.

Nevertheless, the fact that the New Zealand trade minister spoke no Japanese at all meant she had to be close by all the time. Indeed, she found the morning intriguing. The ministers and their aides discussed almost everything but the subject of free trade, which was what had brought both parties here.

Obviously these were just the preliminaries during which each party sized up the other.

Why was she needed at all when Nicholas spoke fluent Japanese, and the Japanese minister equally fluent, if heavily accented, English? Protocol, probably, and the desire not to lose face, and also because a lot could be riding on these preliminaries.

After lunch they spent several hours with the ministers and their cohorts on the rifle range. Nicholas was there, too; he shot well. No doubt he did everything well, she thought, firmly squelching an image of him making love, that lean body poised over hers . . .

Heat shimmered through her, sweet as honey, draining her of energy and common sense.

"No," she muttered, earning herself a startled look from a small, exquisitely dressed Japanese gentleman.

"I wonder what other sports they intend to try?" she said, smiling.

He bowed. "I believe we ride horses," he said politely.

"Oh." She shrugged. "I don't ride," she said.

"Neither do I."

They smiled at each other.

Golf had at least been comparatively quiet, and the links were beautiful—if one excepted the occasional alligator lurking in the ponds. And they were quiet. In spite of the earmuffs they all wore, the rifle range was noisy. Riding, however, threatened to be painful. She was wondering cynically whether she could claim danger pay when Nicholas said, "Clay pigeons next."

Starting, because he'd come up behind her, she met his mocking eyes directly. He couldn't possibly have recognized her boredom because she was an expert at hiding it, so he was just taunting her, seeing how she'd react.

I'll fix him, she thought, and gave him a dazzling, excited smile before obediently accompanying the group to yet more fusillades of noise.

When at last they stopped shooting and returned to the hotel, she had several discussion documents to translate and type while everyone else went to their rooms. Grateful for the reprieve from one particular man's company, she made for the office.

"At least I have reasonable hours," Elise said with commiseration, looking up from her work as Mariel got up and stretched her fingers and back.

"Oh, I get paid well for it. How's Caitlin today?"

"All churned up. I honestly don't know what I'm going to do with her." The older woman put down the sheets of paper she was sorting and pressed her fingertips to her forehead, smoothing out the frown lines toward her temples. "She swears she's going to run away to her father. Says he's going to come and meet her."

Mariel asked tentatively, "Could he be putting ideas in her head?"

"Not as far as I know," Elise said. Looking away, she said bitterly, "She got so upset after he called her the first few times that I told him I wouldn't let her talk on the phone to him anymore because she was unbearable afterward—tantrums and yelling and then crying fit to break her heart."

Preventing any communication at all didn't seem to Mariel to be a good idea, but after a glance at Elise's bleak face she held her tongue. Elise knew her daughter.

The older woman said abruptly, "She still cries in the night and says she's going to see him soon. She misses him, I guess."

"Is she going to spend the holidays with him?"

Elise's mouth clamped shut. "He can't look after her. He's getting a new business off the ground—he's got no time to spend with her. He only sued for custody to teach me a lesson for daring to leave him. It's so typical of him to just go bullheaded for what he wants and never give a thought to how his actions affect anyone else."

"Is he fond of her?"

Elise shrugged. "Yeah, he's fond of her. He even says he loves her, but if loving means you want the other person's happiness above your own, Jimmy's only ever loved himself. The counselor said Caitlin just doesn't know how to deal with the fact that her daddy's left her, so she blames me for it. She hates me working, but she's quite happy staying after school with Saranne Beamish in the village. She likes Saranne's kids. Sometimes I just don't know what to do." Her eyes filled with tears.

"A marriage breakup is always hard on the children, but they get over it," Mariel said soothingly.

From behind came a man's voice, deep and cool and curt. "Have you finished those documents, Mariel?"

She jumped, but not as high as Elise, whose audible gasp sounded loudly in the room.

"No," Mariel said, turning swiftly to shield the older woman from Nicholas's too-observant eyes.

"We need them now," he said.

She nodded. "I'll bring them up to Mr. McCabe when they're done."

"Thank you."

After he'd left, Elise said, "God, he's gorgeous, isn't he? But his eyes send shivers down my spine. I wouldn't like to get on the wrong side of him. Jimmy only bruised my heart. That guy could scar you for life."

"I'm sure he's not violent," Mariel said, shocked.

"There are different sorts of violence," Elise said wearily. "I don't think Tall-dark-and-handsome's cruel by nature, but I'll bet he could be if he was provoked enough. You'd better get on with that work."

The documents were broadly based, without specifics— mere lists of suggestions. After translating them, Mariel took them up to the minister's suite, where she read them through to him, Nicholas and a couple of other men. The older one she recognized with a clutch of foreboding to be a senior diplomat, now retired, whose speciality was Asian affairs. Although he would have known her parents, he showed no signs of identifying her.

That evening each mission was eating separately, no doubt discussing tactics, so her services weren't required. After dinner and a swim in the pool, she spent a couple of hours or so in her room trying to relax, but the shadowy phantoms of her past pressed closer and closer, robbing her of any hope of rest, let alone sleep.

Finally she gave up the effort and crossed to her window and looked out. The moon hung half-blown in the sky, shedding a pale, hazy sheen over the grounds; lights blazed forth from the hotel, but although the paths were still lit by fairy lamps, no one trod between the trees.

She chose tan slacks and a cool cream T-shirt, slipped a soft cream-and-tan sweater over her shoulders and pulled espadrilles onto her feet, then walked outside, wondering just what restless compulsion drove her into the scented darkness.

Urged on by something primal and heartfelt, an unknown goad, she headed toward the beach, remembering other beaches she'd seen, other coasts, other seas far removed from this—seas that beat against rockbound coasts in Norway, seas that lapped blinding coral sands in turquoise lagoons off Fiji, the wild west coast of New Zealand where waves had half the world to gather and build before they fell savagely onto the cliff-bound rim of land.

Odd that New Zealand should come to mind when usually she avoided all thoughts of it.

Well, no, not odd; the image of a face, all aggressive angles, and a lean, disciplined body that moved with predatory grace had been hovering just behind her eyes ever since she'd first seen Nicholas Leigh.

Even as she shivered he appeared, coalescing out of the darkness on the edge of the woods, his head turned to watch her arrive. Not for a moment did she mistake him for anyone else; she had the unsettling feeling that he had brought her there, called her with a primitive, magical lure that had nothing to do with the mundane.

He didn't make any of the usual greetings. As though he had expected her, he held out his hand, and as though he had the right, she gave him hers, this time braced for the jolt of pure awareness that raced through her at his touch.

"You can't see the Southern Cross from here," he said.

"So?"

She caught the quick flash of white as he smiled.

"I was born under the Southern Cross," he said. "I hope to die under it one day."

"Born under it literally?"

"Literally. My parents were sailing when I arrived, too suddenly for them to get back to land. My mother insisted on being on deck. My father said that I looked at the sky as I was born."

Fascinated, she said, "Perhaps you were imprinted like a baby bird."

He laughed softly. "Perhaps. Where were you born, Mariel?"

"In Kashmir," she said, and gave a startled little laugh. "Oddly enough, on a houseboat. I was a month premature."

She kept her eyes on the beach that spread out before them, white in the vaporous moonlight, but she felt his gaze, keen and piercing as a lance of crystal. It kindled an untamed exultation because his reaction was written in his features, and it was just as helpless, just as wild, as hers.

"So you were born on a boat, too."

"Quite a coincidence." Following his lead, she strove to sound matter-of-fact, repressing the astounded excitement that made her feel her whole world was tumbling, racing, shattering, and all she could call on to protect her were the small weapons of her character and willpower.

"A sign, do you think?"

Her attempt at a laugh was blocked somewhere in the region of her heart. "Of what?" she asked. "Careless parents?"

Beneath the amusement in his answering laugh prowled an elemental possessiveness that sent a shiver down her spine. "Perhaps," he said. "A link, anyway."

And because she couldn't allow this, couldn't let him forge connections between them, she said briskly, "Well, both events occurred a long time ago. I'm more interested in the present. Tell me, what happens tomorrow morning? Any possibility of a few exchanges of opinion about trade or barriers or tariffs? I thought they'd be settling into earnest discussions by now."

"Let's sit for a while," he suggested, turning off the hard-packed strand onto the soft powdery sand by the low dunes.

Relieved, she removed her hand from his to sit down, and by doing so felt that in some symbolic way she'd regained a fraction of her autonomy.

Perhaps recognizing the small declaration of independence, he didn't attempt to touch her; instead, he leaned back and looked at the stars. "This is just a preliminary sortie. It's possible that nothing important will actually be discussed this time."

Although he'd followed her change of subject, Mariel detected a note of indulgence in his words, as if he had consciously decided to allow her a breathing space.

"Then why are you all here?" she asked. "This holiday is costing each country a fortune, and all the ministers are doing is running around showing off to each other!"

His smile was brief and ironic. "Both of these men are new to their jobs—they haven't met before. As they're going to be working together, it will make things much simpler if they understand how the other thinks."

"So that's why all the macho posturing," she said with exasperation. "Golf and target shooting. Honestly, when are you men going to give over the world to women and spend all your time playing your childish games without having the affairs of the world hinge on them? That way you wouldn't do nearly so much damage."

To her astonishment he laughed again. "Oh, I agree heartily, but diplomacy is conducted along different lines."

With eyes adjusted to the night, Mariel looked at him shrewdly. "You don't sound as though you buy into the ethos."

His smile remained, the amusement in his expression didn't alter, but she knew as plainly as if she'd seen it that her words had struck some hidden tender spot.

"I'm a diplomat, so I must," he said evenly. "I agree it can be slow and sometimes infuriating, but often it works. Building a personal bridge can help."

Recognizing the evasion, she decided to pin this irritatingly elusive man down. "What exactly is your part in all this posturing?"

"My area of expertise is trade."

Of course, he was a diplomat, and they were experts at avoiding the issue. "So what," she demanded, "beyond finding out that Mr. Watanabe is the better golfer and Mr. McCabe the better shot, do any of you expect to learn from this expensive exercise?"

"I don't expect to learn anything," he said calmly. "I am a mere cog in the wheel, the lowliest of the low."

She laughed, she couldn't help it, the sound clear and low and warm in the salty air. "You don't look the sort of man to indulge in mock humility," she retorted.

"Mock humility I can manage," he assured her. "I have been told that the real stuff is beyond me."

A note in the deep voice snagged her attention. Whoever had told him that had been a woman. Stung, she said mordantly, "I believe it," as she got to her feet.

With the automatic courtesy she was beginning to expect, he rose, too. In the shifting veils of moonlight his eyes glinted, and she thought with a sudden chill that trading insults with this man could be a dangerous pastime.

"I'd better go back," she murmured.

"Ah, yes, I'd forgotten that you're not expected to mingle with the guests."

"Well, the resort doesn't pay me to sit around discovering the inner workings of the diplomatic mind," she retorted crisply.

"Don't they allow you time off?"

"Of course they do, but I'm still on the other side of the divide."

"Are you an employee?"

He'd have found out all about her before recommending that she take the other interpreter's place, so why the questions? She sent him a swift sideways glance, but his face was unreadable.

"No, free-lance. An agency in New York organizes my jobs for me."

"And you enjoy your work?"

"Love it," she said firmly.

"You're extremely good at it. You have both McCabe and Watanabe eating out of your hand."

How did he do it? He wasn't even looking at her, yet her skin pulled tight and she had the unnerving sensation of being totally, completely scrutinized—absorbed, taken in, everything about her measured and assessed.

"They both have a charming, old-fashioned courtesy," she said dryly.

"The Japanese say you speak their language like a native."

To satisfy his probing curiosity she said serenely, "When I lived in Tokyo my parents sent me to a Japanese school. In a situation like that you learn fast, believe me. Of course, the year I spent back in Japan when I was eighteen helped refine my accent."

"And did you live in China and France as a child?"

She smiled, striving so hard for a casual unaffected air that her throat ached. "Hong Kong," she said. "And for a while I had a French governess who was forbidden to speak English to me."

"Peripatetic parents," he said, his lashes drooping to hide his thoughts.

"Very," she returned steadily. "Nomads."

Just how nomadic their life had been she hadn't realized until she went back to New Zealand, a shocked, bewildered eight-year-old plunged into the narrow, restrictive society of a small, unsympathetic country town. Two things had saved her—a kindly neighbor who provided her with uncritical affection, and an extremely good language teacher at the local high school who had seen her talents and helped her regain the languages she had almost lost.

"If I'm to be any good tomorrow I'd better go now," she said, infusing her voice with a brisk, no-nonsense tone.

"Very well, then." He sounded amused, as though he recognized her retreat but was prepared to allow her to run from him for the time being, because the result was never in doubt.

CHAPTER THREE

HE WAS TOO BLOODY ARROGANT for his own good, she thought confusedly as she paced along the sand beside his tall presence.

As they were crossing the low band of scrub and palmettos that bordered the beach, something rustled in the bushes. Nicholas moved instantly, sidestepping swiftly so that he was between her and the noise.

"It's nothing," she said, surprised. "Perhaps a squirrel."

"There are snakes here."

She laughed. "And like all New Zealanders you're paranoid about them. Don't worry, the night is cool enough to keep them fairly lethargic. It's not likely to be an alligator, either. They prefer the golf course. It could be a raccoon."

His eyes gleamed as he looked down at her. "Snakes don't worry you?"

"No, I'm used to them." He didn't deny his attitude, which secretly impressed her. But then he wasn't the sort of man whose self-esteem demanded that he pretend invulnerability; he didn't need the false confidence of bravado.

He kept walking, but she noticed that he stayed alert until they got back to the staff quarters. There he smiled at her and said, "Sleep well."

She willed herself to relax, but that tingling in her skin and the sensitive reaction between her shoulder blades told her that he watched her until the door closed behind her.

Damn, she thought. He *was* curious, and for a moment her heart quailed. Then she straightened and went to her room. It was stupid to get into a tizz; he was probably just interested because she was a New Zealander.

Was he security? No, he was too obvious. Security men tended to be inconspicuous, part of their usefulness being their ability to fade into the background. Nicholas Leigh, she thought grimly, would fade into no background; there was something about him that made everyone notice him. When he walked into a room people looked, their attention caught whether they wanted it to be or not.

And she didn't. She might be so attracted to him that her body sang when he was near, but she couldn't afford to let anything happen. Ah, well, just another three days...

But that night she dreamed of him—explicit, erotic dreams that shocked her and made her feel as though another woman inhabited her skin, a woman whose fantasies had taken over her sleep. Even in her one serious relationship she had never dreamed like that, and David had been a good lover, thoughtful, tender and gentle.

Unfortunately gentleness had played no part in her dreams, and she awoke with the appalled realization that some hitherto unsuspected part of her had recognized and responded to an elemental savagery in Nicholas Leigh.

Daylight, of course, brought better counsel. She neither believed that violence was a part of love, nor accepted that love meant forgiving violent tendencies, so her dreams had to be some aberration born of the hazy magic of a South Carolina moon and her vulnerability to Nicholas's smoldering animal magnetism.

"Grit your teeth," she told her reflection, "and tough it out, because once this is over you're never going to see him again."

Her reflection grimaced back, blue eyes slitted, full mouth pursed in a mock pout.

"Oh, just get on with it," she said crossly, smoothing an unruly lock of hair behind her ear. "You're an adult, for heaven's sake. You're no shrinking little virgin to be thrilled into a man's bed. It's sexual attraction, pure and simple, and it's not going to do either of you any good because in this day and age people don't sleep with strangers. Even if they want to. Which I don't. So stop thinking about the man."

It wasn't much to ask of her willpower, after all.

"And tell yourself another lie," she scoffed as she turned away from the mirror. "I wonder what they plan to do today? Play bridge, perhaps."

But the ministers went out fishing on a large, white boat. Because the Japanese interpreter was on duty, Mariel intended to spend the day helping Elise, but Mr. McCabe saw her walking through the foyer as the party came down and insisted gallantly that she go with them.

"That's very kind of you," she said, "but I can't—"

"Nonsense," he said cheerfully. "Just what you need. A few hours at sea will blow the cobwebs out."

So she acquiesced with a graceful smile, only to be unreasonably cross because Nicholas wasn't one of the party.

Conversation that morning was more personal. While the ministers sat side by side watching for strikes, they discussed books and a play both had seen in Geneva. They mentioned their families, a daughter who wished to be a lawyer, a son who had already joined the diplomatic service, another who was at university.

They talked sports, and here there came a breakthrough. Both men discovered that they shared an interest in swords, the New Zealand minister an aficionado of foils, the Japanese a practitioner—very humble, very poor, he assured his opposite—of the arcane art of samurai swordsmanship.

Within moments both she and the Japanese interpreter were at full stretch, neither fully at home with such an esoteric subject, helping each other out with words and phrases. Fishing forgotten, the glitter of the sea ignored, both ministers settled down to explore the differing techniques of their respective skills. It was patently obvious that they were enjoying themselves enormously.

Mariel began to understand the reasoning behind the days spent on the island.

After lunch she slipped along to the business centre, only to be told by Elise that there was nothing for her to do.

"Go and rest," the older woman advised.

"I spent all morning out at sea on a huge boat."

"Interpreting, no doubt. Go for a walk. The pathway around the golf course is just lovely at this time of year, with all the azaleas in flower."

It certainly sounded idyllic, so Mariel took her advice. There, for the first time that day, she saw Nicholas—playing in a foursome with both ministers and another aide. Hidden in the shade of a vine-covered trellis, she narrowed her eyes against the sunlight and watched them tee off, trying to pin down as dispassionately as she could exactly what stopped the breath in her throat whenever she saw Nicholas Leigh.

It wasn't as though she hadn't met better-looking men. A French film star came to mind, a man who looked like a god come to earth, but in spite of his interest in her, she hadn't been able to feel anything more than the respect supreme beauty always demands.

Whereas, she acknowledged wryly, she'd find it very hard to resist Nicholas's dark, dominating magnetism.

If power was as great an aphrodisiac as it was supposed to be, she'd be watching the ministers. However, it was Nicholas who sent the blood racing through her veins in a feverish, consuming disquietude. Although it was humiliating to admit it, his combination of virile masculinity and ice-cold intelligence excited her.

You're developing masochistic tendencies, she thought scornfully. *And that's a dangerous way to go.*

Behind her, conversation announced the slow perambulation of people on the pathway that ran beside the golf course. They stopped on the other side of the trellis with its burden of sweetly smelling flowers. Mariel couldn't see who they were and didn't want to proclaim her presence, but their voices declared their origins to be New Zealand.

"Just look at the Golden Boy," one said, his tone an unpleasant mixture of envy and dislike. Peter Sanderson. "Showing off his muscles and his expensive clothes and his superb style."

The other man said curiously, "You really hate him, don't you? What's he done to you?"

"He walks in with a Ph.D. no better than mine and gets a job that's going places, doesn't work at the coal face like the rest of us. Oh, no, he's immediately bumped three steps up the latter. It's bloody unfair."

"Come on, now *you're* being a bit unfair. He's got the brains—even you can't deny that—and he seems to have an instinctive knowledge of how the system works, as well as being damned good at his job. Of course it doesn't harm his chances that he's also got so much charisma it's coming out his ears."

"Charisma." Peter Sanderson made it an obscenity. "All that means is he's got looks that send stupid women into a flutter, the money to buy clothes and the arrogance that comes with a silver spoon in your mouth and really useful, rich connections. Take those away and what is there?"

Laughing, the second man stated, "Initiative, determination, decisiveness and a damned good brain, as well as the sort of self-discipline that makes you grit your teeth, subtlety, and a cool, patrician understanding of humanity's weaknesses."

"Stuck-up—!"

The profanity made Mariel blink.

Sanderson continued with a passionate intensity that lifted the hairs on the back of her neck. "What really bugs me is that it's all been so easy for him."

His companion said, "It hasn't always been easy. His family circumstances were irregular, to say the least."

"Oh, I know he's a bastard, but he's old Philip Leigh's bastard, and Philip Leigh was the richest man in New Zealand when he was killed in that motorway pileup. I also know that, apart from a trust for his wife, Philip Leigh left everything to Nicholas."

"Yeah, well, Rosemary Clifford—Nicholas's mother— made sure of that." The second man added reminiscently, "I met her once. She'd have been in her late forties, but I tell you, she made my hormones surge into overdrive! Man, she was everything anyone would want in a woman. It was no wonder she led old Philip around by the nose. Talk about oozing sex from every pore—and yet she wasn't some cheap bimbo. I thought of geishas—you know, the proper ones— and the courtesans of ancient Greece. Brains, looks, personality and talent, she had it all. And class. Philip Leigh was a hard businessman, a brilliant man, but apart from that he didn't have much personality. She obviously stuck with him for the money."

"She couldn't persuade him to divorce his wife and legalize her illegitimate son," Sanderson said maliciously.

"I wonder if she tried. She struck me as being supremely satisfied with her life. After all, she had the power and she knew it. Nicholas was the only child and, therefore, bastard or not, Philip's heir."

"I wouldn't mind an upbringing like that." The acrid note in Sanderson's voice chilled Mariel. She moved slightly, not wanting to hear any more yet unable to get away without being observed.

"Okay, so you had it tough, but look at it this way. You've climbed the ladder the hard way, and don't think you aren't valued for it."

"Like a monkey using a stick for a tool," Peter Sanderson retorted bitterly. "Everyone says, well, it's not a great trick, but who'd have thought the stupid thing had the brains to work it out?"

"That sounds like an inferiority complex to me."

"Inferiority complexes tend to be inherent in people born on the wrong side of the tracks," Sanderson said. "Oh, don't take any notice of me. I'm just venting my working-class spleen. But I'll tell you one thing, it would make my life much more satisfying if I could get just one small piece of dirt on Golden Boy out there, something that would wipe the smug look from his aristocratic face. Nobody can be as perfect as he is. Being a bastard should do it—twenty years ago it would've been a real black mark, but somehow he's managed to convince everyone to overlook it. Come on, we'd better go."

The second man said as they moved off, "You're going to have to do something about this irrational dislike you've developed, because Nicholas is heading straight for the top, and you don't want to find yourself unable to work with him."

His companion said something, the angry resentment in his voice obvious although his words weren't. Disturbed, Mariel's frowning gaze fixed on Nicholas as he walked down the fairway. It wasn't too surprising that he had an enemy—his brand of potent masculinity and authority was bound to grate on anyone with a fragile ego—but the news that he was the product of an adulterous affair was intriguing.

There must be scars, although it was impossible to imagine Nicholas allowing anyone to see them. He would hate to know that these two men had been discussing him, she thought shrewdly. He gave the impression of being an intensely private person, hiding his emotions behind an armor so seamless that it would take a bomb to get through.

And why should she be concerned? Physical attraction was involuntary and couldn't be helped, but it was risky to begin to wonder about a man. It left you open to fantasies, and indulging in daydreams could be a dangerous, will-sapping business.

Turning, she brushed past the vine and walked back down the path.

In the office Elise frowned. "Hardly a walk," she commented, ostentatiously looking at her watch.

"It's getting fairly warm out there now. Haven't you got some work for me to do?"

"Well, all right, if you really want to. This pile of typing has just arrived from one of the cottages down toward the lighthouse. Some media mogul can't let a day go by without working."

Between the two of them they finished the pile in an hour.

"Thanks, Mariel," Elise said, checking through the last document. "What's your delegation doing?"

Mariel stood up and stacked the sheets of paper into a neat pile. "Playing golf again."

"Some people have it easy," the older woman said on a sigh. "I'm supposed to be organizing a birthday party for Caitlin. She's eight today."

"McDonald's?"

Elise rolled her eyes. "Bite your tongue! Here? On this sacred ground, this hallowed turf? The Jermains would die rather than allow a franchise operation on the island. If the islanders want to eat fast food, they have to go over to the mainland."

Mariel laughed. "Why are you here if it's Caitlin's birthday? Where's Tina?" she asked, referring to the woman who helped when the office was busy and acted as backup in Elise's absence.

"She called in sick, and there was no one else so I had to come." Elise stretched, pushing her hands into the small of her back. "It's all right, I've only got a few last-minute things to do, and Caitlin's with Saranne. At the moment it seems she'd rather be with anyone but me."

The telephone rang; after answering it she handed it over to Mariel, mouthing, "He sounds mad."

Apparently the golf game was over, for it was Nicholas Leigh, and although he didn't sound exactly angry, he was certainly at his most crisp. "Could you come up to my room straight away, please. Bring your computer," he said, and hung up.

"Yes, it is a lovely day," Mariel said sweetly and childishly as she replaced the receiver.

"Trouble?"

She shrugged. "It had better not be."

HE WAS STANDING by the window looking down at the smooth sweep of lawns, his brows drawn together. In one lean hand were two sheets of paper.

When she knocked on the open door he swung around and focused on her, the brilliant eyes glittering. "Ah, Mariel," he said, a note of sarcasm hardening his tone. "I have a letter here I'd like you to translate."

All business. No sign of the man from last night, the man who'd held her hand, moved so quickly to put himself between her and a possible danger.

She was glad. It was much safer this way. And the sooner she got it done, the quicker she'd be out of here.

The fax was a reply from the Japanese industrialist. Mariel wondered whether he knew that Nicholas was illegitimate.

Probably, and it wouldn't matter. Even the most hidebound and conventional society would take Nicholas Leigh on his own valuation.

But it was interesting that Nicholas, who was a diplomat and therefore shouldn't have ties with any commercial enterprise, dealt with business for a trust presumably set up by his father. Surely diplomats were supposed to be totally impartial.

Peter Sanderson might just find the "dirt" he was looking for. Well, he wouldn't find it out from her. Swiftly taking the letter from the printer, she handed it to Nicholas.

"What's the matter?"

She looked up, her eyes widening a fraction. "Nothing."

"Did you enjoy the conversation you overheard by the golf course?"

Color roiled up through her skin, heating her cheekbones and throat. Composedly she replied, "Not in the least."

"I imagine it was a diatribe against me."

"Do all your fellow workers dislike you?" she asked in her most interested tone.

He showed his teeth in an unimpressed smile. "Sanderson certainly does."

"I gather it's a personality conflict," she said neutrally. "It happens all the time."

"The essence of discretion," he mocked, his gaze disturbingly direct.

"It goes with the job," she returned, lifting her chin a fraction. "As you're well aware. I'm quite sure you read my dossier carefully before deciding to co-opt me."

He acknowledged the hit with a slight smile. "You appear to have led a remarkably blameless life."

With far from blameless parents, she thought.

"I don't know of anyone with a blameless life," she said casually, smiling, willing her expression to be calm and clear and candid. "Do you need me anymore?"

"No, thank you." He looked down at her translation, and she felt his attention shift as though she no longer registered. "Close the door on your way out, will you?" he asked absently.

She did, and came face-to-face with Peter Sanderson on his way down the corridor. He stopped, his gaze intent and astonished. Mariel knew she looked guilty—a combination of her unwitting eavesdropping that morning and the mention of his name a few moments ago—but guilty or not, that was no excuse for the rapid shift in his expression from surprise to knowingness and then to salacious interest.

"Don't mind me," he said, looking from her to the door. "Sorry I came along at an inopportune time."

Mariel could feel the color begin to lick along her cheekbones. She didn't make the mistake of trying to excuse herself; instead, she smiled, gripped the handles of her computer bag to thrust it forward into his line of sight and said graciously, "I'm sure you could never come along at an inopportune time, sir. Do you want to see Mr. Leigh? He's in."

"No, no," he said hastily, still looking her over, and laughed.

The door opened behind her. Nicholas said irritably, "What's going on here?"

"I thought Mr. Sanderson wanted to see you," Mariel explained, aware of the instant chill in the atmosphere.

The older man said smoothly, "I just happened to be on my way to the minister's suite when Miss—ah—"

"Browning," she supplied evenly.

"Yes, well, when Miss Browning came out of your room."

Nicholas's brows lifted. He looked down at Mariel, and something flamed in the green-gold eyes, something that almost made her duck, before he transferred his gaze to the other man. "Do you want to speak to me?"

"No, no, not at all."

"Then perhaps," Nicholas said with freezing courtesy, "you and Ms. Browning could conduct your conversation somewhere else?"

Peter Sanderson's eyes flickered. In spite of everything, Mariel felt sorry for him; she could read his chagrin as clearly as she could feel her own indignation at Nicholas's cavalier dismissal.

"I must go," she said, smiling impartially at both men.

Nicholas met her smile with a cold austerity that failed entirely to hide his anger. Why was he so furious?

With an erect back and stiffly held head, she walked past him and set off for the staircase, only to be distracted as the Sanderson man called, "Wait a minute. I'll come down with you."

The last thing she wanted was his company, but she wasn't going to make it obvious. So she slowed, listening to the soft thunk as Nicholas closed the door into his room, and made herself smile as the shorter man caught up with her near the staircase.

Gritting her teeth, Mariel produced a pale smile. He was crowding her, his gaze lingering too long on her face.

"It's an interesting old house, isn't it?" she said.

"I think it's damn inconvenient. I mean, for a start there're no lifts. Still, I suppose some people like this sort of thing."

"Yes, some of us do. I always enjoy coming to Bride's Bay Resort," she said sedately.

"Do you come here often?"

"I've been here several times."

"Where did you live in New Zealand before you broke hearts by moving off?" he asked with an attempt at urbanity.

"In the King Country," she told him.

"Then we're probably related," he said, and when she looked up, startled, he gave her a sly smile. "I've got relatives in Te Kuiti. The Sparrows. Do you know them? No, it's not likely." The glance that accompanied this managed to combine appreciation of the way she looked with resentment. "Don't look so surprised. You must know that most New Zealanders are either related or have lived next door to each other. Are you from diplomatic circles, Mariel?"

"No," she said levelly, not daring to trust her voice to more than the monosyllable.

"Oh, I thought you were."

Swallowing surreptitiously, she asked, "Why?"

"I'm sure I heard someone say you seemed familiar, but perhaps it's just a general Kiwi aura. Although I don't know of many New Zealanders who look like you—I wish there were more!"

She didn't like his heavy-handed gallantry, but common courtesy brought a smile to her lips. "You're very kind," she said automatically, and turned toward the back of the hotel.

"Where are you off to?"

"The business centre, Mr. Sanderson. I'm on duty."

"Oh. I thought we might have a drink."

So he could pump her some more, no doubt. "I'm sorry, we aren't supposed to drink with the guests."

His face went rigid for all the world as though she had insulted him. Then he seemed to relax. "Only with Nicholas Leigh," he said a little too heartily.

Mariel's brows shot up. "And even then," she said gently, "only when ordered to."

For a moment he looked taken aback, until disbelief overrode it. "I wonder why he did that," he said in a significant tone. "I suppose I could always order you to have one with me."

It took an effort, but she managed to keep her voice pleasantly polite. "We were discussing business. And it was the minister who ordered it, not Ni—Mr. Leigh."

His shoulders moved. "Oh, I see," he said buoyantly, still smiling, although she could see the wheels revolving in his brain. "Are you on duty tonight?"

She nodded, hiding her unease. "Yes."

"Then I'll see you at dinner."

Her smile was becoming mechanical, but she said, "Of course," and walked away from him. That driven intensity worried her. Such men had the potential for instability, especially when they took every rebuff, even one as courteously delivered as hers had been, personally.

Down at the golf course, his dislike of Nicholas had seemed mere ranting; now she took it more seriously. And although it was ridiculous, she wished she hadn't been coming out of Nicholas's room as he was passing by.

Why had Nicholas been so angry when he opened the door and saw them talking together?

The query stayed with her all through the afternoon. From somewhere, the hotel had managed to rustle up a set of foils and two heavy, decorative and superbly balanced weapons that she recognized as Samurai swords. Just another example of the service for which Bride's Bay was famous, Mariel thought with irony.

With the anticipation of children promised a treat, both ministers went off to the gym in the spa to indulge in a spot of swordplay.

The two men had a great time, showing off a little, admiring and then attempting to learn something of each other's arcane art. Mariel was fascinated, because, in spite of some swift swotting in her Japanese dictionary, Mr. Watanabe used terms she'd never come across before, and there was nothing she enjoyed more than furthering her skills.

Red-faced and sweating, they eventually decided to call a halt, to the not-quite-concealed relief of the two security men—one Japanese, the other a member of the New Zealand delegation—who had watched the bouts with the same stony faces. They'd probably spent the entire time, Mariel thought with a small, inner smile, composing excuses to use with their superiors if one of the ministers managed to pink the other.

As she didn't know whether she'd be needed further, Mariel wandered across to the window to wait while the ministers showered. Moving purposefully, the New Zealand security man joined her. Middle-aged, with the hard-bitten lack of distinction that served his kind so well, he had sharp eyes.

"I keep thinking I know you," he said without preamble. "Have we met before?"

An icy needle of caution worked its way down her spine. "I don't think so, but it's not impossible. I do a lot of this sort of work, although it's usually with businessmen."

"Do you work at the United Nations?"

"I have, but not lately." Not since David.

He frowned. "I'd have thought that would be more lucrative than free-lancing."

"There's not as much variety," she said noncommittally. "I like to travel."

Eyes never leaving her face, he nodded. She didn't know whether he was deliberately trying to intimidate her, or whether this was his normal manner.

"Perhaps I saw you there," he said, but without much conviction. "Although I keep thinking I've seen your photograph."

She shrugged. "I doubt it. They usually clear the interpreters away when it comes to taking photos. Unless it's been a photo on an ID tag somewhere." From somewhere she summonded a light laugh. "On the other hand, you've probably gone through Howard Forsythe's files. He has dossiers on everyone, and I'm sure mine has a shocking photo."

Howard Forsythe was the head of security at the resort.

"Yes, that's probably it," the New Zealander said.

Relieved, she saw the ministers come back into the room. "Here they are," she said, adding, "I spent the afternoon hoping neither of them had a heart attack."

He closed his eyes briefly. "Don't even think of it," he said as they both moved toward the two men.

Some hours later, in the foyer, she saw him earnestly talking to Sanderson. As she moved to let Mr. McCabe walk in front of her, Sanderson looked up, and she realized from some small change in his expression that she was the subject of their conversation.

Banishing the tumbling seeds of worry from her mind, she forced her attention back to the man who spoke to her. "I won't need you any more this evening," the minister said, smiling.

Although he was a politician, he was a nice man.

"Thank you for your efforts this afternoon." His smile widened into a grin. "When you took up interpreting I don't suppose you ever thought you'd find yourself discussing the more esoteric points of seventeenth-century Samurai swordplay."

"No, sir, I didn't," she said. "It was fascinating."

He looked at her with benign shrewdness. "Was it? I'll bet you were bored to tears." He looked around. "Definitely above and beyond the call of duty. Ah, Nicholas."

And he materialized, tall and overpowering, the lights warming his hair to bronze, green-gold eyes self-possessed above his hard, arrogantly outlined mouth. Mariel willed her smile to hold steady.

"Nicholas, why don't you take Ms. Browning out to dinner?" the minister suggested. "It's too early for her to go to bed."

"Oh, but—"

"I'd very much like that," Nicholas interrupted blandly. He nodded to Mariel, those eyes holding her prisoner. "If you don't mind waiting, Ms. Browning, until I see someone?"

She did mind, but faced with the minister's cheerful smile of complicity—did he know how she felt whenever Nicholas Leigh came within sight of her?—she had to stay there.

"Not at all," she said courteously. She waited until he left them before saying, "I am on duty this evening, Mr. McCabe."

"We don't need you." Observing Nicholas's tall, lithe figure as he made his way across the room, the minister confided, "He'll go far, that man. A brilliant future—ambassador material at the very least. I wouldn't be surprised if you interpret his speech at the United Nations one day."

"Neither would I," Mariel murmured, not knowing what else to say.

"He was a Rhodes Scholar at Oxford, you know. Ph.D., great athlete and a leader. Yes, the world's his oyster."

Mariel said neutrally, "Rather overwhelming." Of course the world was his oyster; the only children of very rich men grew up with an inborn confidence that swept everything before them.

The older man's astute gaze came to rest on her carefully composed face. "Very attractive to the opposite sex, I believe, but not a womanizer."

Why was he telling her this? She called up her most remote expression and said woodenly, "That would be a massive character flaw."

"Absolutely." The minister surveyed Nicholas's returning form. "A very clever man. Just like his father."

Nicholas had heard the comment, as perhaps he was meant to. Nothing altered in the hard, compelling face, but Mariel wondered why he objected to being compared to his father.

Her conviction was reinforced when the minister said, "I was just telling Mariel how like your father you are."

In a completely colorless voice Nicholas returned, "You flatter me."

"Nonsense." The minister smiled. "He was a good man, your father, did a lot for New Zealand." He gave a short nod, said his good-nights and walked briskly with his small entourage across the floor.

Nicholas looked down at Mariel, his eyes glittering like jewels beneath his lashes. He was, she realized with a shock, starkly, uncompromisingly furious. "Let's go," he said.

Silently she accompanied him out of the room, but once they were out of sight she said politely, "He seems to think

I need entertaining, and really, I don't. I certainly don't want to feel that I'm imposing on you. Or being imposed on you."

"You know better than that," he returned lightly. His mouth curved in a mirthless parody of a smile. "Neither of us has an option. We've been more or less ordered to go out to dinner together, and I'm a good corporate player."

No protestations that he'd enjoy it, that he hadn't been shanghaied into it. Piqued, even though she was telling herself that at least he wasn't a hypocrite, she snapped, "I find that hard to believe."

"Why?"

"Oh, merely that you seem to be the sort of person who makes up his own mind about things rather than letting other people make the decisions."

"Eventually," he said with an assurance that set her blinking, "I intend to be the one making the decisions."

"You'd have to be a politician to do that." Her voice was edged with a fine scorn.

He said on a note of mockery, "I gather you don't think much of politicians."

"I like Mr. McCabe."

"An intelligent man, and one who has the welfare of his country truly at heart," he agreed dispassionately. "Come on, Mariel. We'll have a drink first and then go in to dinner."

She hesitated, but the gleam of determination in his eyes warned her it would be simpler if she just gave in and went with him.

Besides, humiliating though it was, she wanted to.

They had almost reached the staircase when the security man who had spoken to her in the gym came up and said to Nicholas, "I'm sorry, can I see you for a moment? Alone, I'm afraid."

At Nicholas's frown Mariel said swiftly, "It's all right, I'll wait here."

Nicholas gave a sharp nod and walked off with the security guard farther down the corridor. Mariel looked down at the antique desk against the wall, with its skillfully arranged bouquet of flowers and clever placement of objets d'art, trying to hide the cold dread in her stomach.

Somehow she wasn't surprised when she heard Peter Sanderson say, "Ah, there you are, Mariel."

Fatuous remark, she thought, trying hard not to dislike him. Of course she was there. Turning, she smiled.

His glance flicked from her face to her hands, sideways, and then back to her face again. "I wondered whether you'd like to come to a nightclub on the mainland tonight," he said, adding, "Several of us decided we needed a chance to let our hair down. And as it appears you are not on duty after all..."

Nicholas had left the security man and was striding toward them, his expression set in formidable lines. Hastily Mariel said, "I'm sorry, I—"

"Ms. Browning and I are going to dinner," Nicholas interrupted. He smiled down at the shorter man and said with a pleasantness that was intended to be offensive, "However, it was a nice thought, Sanderson. Perhaps we'll join you later."

For a moment Mariel thought the other man would respond to this gratuitous patronage with an explosion, but although the effort was obvious he managed to rein in his temper. He even smiled, saying, "My loss, then. Good evening," and left them with his dignity more or less intact.

"That," Mariel said as Nicholas slipped his hand under her elbow and turned her toward the stairs, "was egregiously rude. You're a diplomat—you're supposed to know how to behave."

"I don't like poachers."

"He didn't know. And I don't like being compared to a rabbit or a pigeon—I'm not prey."

"Aren't you?" His smile was chilling, impersonal. "I think you are—soft and tender prey, very elusive and enigmatic, always on your guard." He paused, and then continued, "I have no right to ask this or even suggest it, but I'd keep away from Peter Sanderson if I were you. He doesn't do things without an ulterior motive."

Mariel shrugged. "Perhaps he just likes the look of me," she said coolly. "Men do, I find. It's something to do with the reputation redheads invariably get landed with. I'm sure Ms. Waterhouse could tell you how very irritating it can be."

"Of course he likes the look of you," Nicholas said obliquely. "However, he dislikes me enough to make that a secondary consideration."

"The last thing I want," she said with quick forcefulness, "is to get caught up in the feud you appear to be fanning so assiduously."

"Anything for a quiet life?" His tone told her that he didn't believe it. "Yet you look like someone who has already been at the heart of more storms than most women enjoy in a lifetime."

CHAPTER FOUR

HER HEART SQUEEZED still. Surely he didn't know—if he did he wouldn't be directing enigmatic comments at her. He'd be confronting her with the facts.

Warmed by the returning pulse of life through her veins, Mariel found herself wishing that fate didn't have such a black sense of humor. Of all the talents she could have been born with it was ironic that hers was one that periodically brought her into such close proximity with diplomats.

Although the bar was full, the conversation was generally muted, only occasionally punctuated by laughter. Mariel smiled at the bartender, a young man being trained to the most exacting standards by Desmond, nodded soberly at Desmond as he took in her escort with a serious look, and allowed herself to be seated.

"He doesn't approve," Nicholas said when Desmond had taken their order. His eyes glinted in the subdued lighting. "The hotel must be very strict about fraternizing. Will you get into trouble?"

"No, I'm not an employee, and anyway, Liz Jermain knows I don't make a habit of drinking in the bar—with or without guests. If anyone does tell tales, she'll know I'm here for the same reason you are, because your boss told you to ask me."

He leaned back, scanning her face with a smile at once sardonic and interested. "Does that rankle?"

"Not in the least," she said calmly.

"So, tell me why you don't see me as a pattern diplomat. Apart from my tongue, of course."

She said uneasily, "I don't recollect saying that, exactly."

"That was what you meant."

"Oh, I suppose it's because you're more...noticeable than most diplomats," she said crossly, irritated with him for pinning her down.

"Noticeable?"

Good. She'd surprised him. "Diplomats are usually like security men," she said, giving caution the toss. "They develop the ability to blend into the background. I doubt very much whether there's any background that would let you blend into it. You stand out, you make waves, people watch you when you come into a room. They listen to you automatically without questioning your right to talk. Those are not diplomatic attributes, although I'm sure if anyone can turn them into assets, you can. And when you lose your temper that smooth, assured judiciousness goes out the window." She couldn't prevent the slight twist of cynicism in her tone.

"You've been reading too many romantic novels," he said caustically.

Delighted that her observation had loosened his grip on his self-sufficient perch, she grinned. "I read them," she admitted cheerfully. "I read lots of other things, too. And you haven't addressed the issue—excellent diversionary tactics."

A humorless smile barely lifted the corners of his mouth. "Just for the record," he said, his very lack of emphasis catching her attention more swiftly than a shout would have, "I've wanted to be a diplomat since I was about twelve. In fact, I can't remember ever wanting to be anything else."

"Not even the driver of a fire engine?"

His smile didn't warm. In the dim light of the bar the shadows claimed him so that he was all hard edges and angles, his eyes gleaming beneath dark lashes, his hair black, his skin swarthy copper. "Not that I can remember," he said. "But then, my mother would probably have had a fit if any child of hers had suggested such a plebian ambition."

Memories of the overheard conversation about his childhood circumstances surfaced like scum on a pond. Mariel said hastily, "You haven't any brothers and sisters, I believe."

"No." He knew she'd heard gossip; she could tell by the swift whiplash of a glance he gave her, but his expression didn't alter. "Do you?"

"I was an only child, too," she said. Plowing heavily on, she asked, "Do you like your job?"

"It satisfies my idealistic streak," he said offhandedly. "Common sense tells me that whatever I do adds only a small amount to the sum of human happiness, but at least it's on the side of good. I do my best. It uses all my intelligence, keeps me at full stretch. I can't think of any other career that would do that for me."

Perhaps not, and yet, she thought as the drinks arrived, she could. She had absolutely no doubt that he'd be a success at anything he wanted to do, but for some reason she felt diplomacy was not his métier. Although he wore the attributes of power with controlled panache, when she looked at him she saw a buccaneer.

A voice from behind said, "There you are, Nicholas. I've been looking for you." It was a feminine voice, even and crisp and controlled.

Susan Waterhouse, Mariel saw as Nicholas got to his feet.

"Ah, Ms. Browning," Susan said, smiling coolly. "I'm sorry, I shouldn't interrupt, but I've done something rather stupid and I wonder if I could just borrow Nicholas for a minute or so to tell me how to rescue myself."

Mariel smiled back, but said nothing.

"I won't be a moment," Nicholas told her, and escorted the other woman to the far side of the room, where they stood for some moments. Mariel tried to keep her eyes off the two of them but couldn't help noticing that Susan did most of the talking, and that no expression escaped from Nicholas's hard face.

She had almost finished her glass of mineral water when he came back.

"Sorry," he said calmly.

Mariel carefully didn't look at him. "That's all right."

"If you've finished your drink," Nicholas said, "we have a table waiting for us in the restaurant."

He had procured the most intimate table in the hotel dining room, which specialized in classic low-country cuisine. Mariel had never been in it before, so she looked appreciatively around the Wedgwood blue room, admiring the tables with their white linen damask tablecloths and napkins starched so stiffly they almost crackled. Tall white candles were wreathed with azalea flowers the same pinks and golds and reds as the Victorian posies on the elaborate china.

"It's lovely," she said.

"It has," Nicholas responded, "an excellent reputation."

And enormous prices! Just as well his father had been a very rich man.

The food was magnificent; making a mental reminder to congratulate the kitchen staff, Mariel ate she-crab soup and a wonderful stew of chicken, shrimp and sausage, while slowly drinking two glasses of glorious wine, one French, one Californian.

"I don't think I've ever eaten anything more delicious," she sighed.

"South Carolina is noted for its superb food. But then, you must know that—you've been here before, haven't you?"

"Yes, quite regularly over the years. I've eaten she-crab soup before," she said, "and it was good, but here it was absolutely out of this world. As for this magnificent chocolate mousse...words fail me!"

He was laughing at her, and she suddenly realized that until that moment he had been taut with some hidden emotion. Perhaps because the wine had loosened her tongue, she gave him a slow, languorous smile and said mischievously, "There's nothing in New Zealand like this!"

His lashes drooped, hiding his thoughts, then lifted suddenly to reveal the cool jade of his eyes. "Not exactly like this," he admitted, "but we are developing an interesting cuisine, a sort of combination of Mediterranean and Asian styles on a bedrock of British cuisine. How long did you say it is since you've been home?"

"Home? I don't really think of New Zealand as home—more like three little islands hanging off the end of the world." Afraid she had revealed too much, she called her unruly tongue to order. "Ten years," she said.

"You should go back, you know. You might have grown up enough to appreciate it."

She shrugged. "Perhaps. It always seemed so...circumscribed."

"I suppose it would after a childhood spent wandering some of the more exotic byways of the world. Were you teased at school in that little town in the backblocks?"

"Oh, yes. To which I reacted badly."

"A crybaby?" he mocked gently.

She shook her head. "No. If I'd been able to cry, it might have been all right, but I wouldn't do it. I refused to give them the satisfaction, and of course they teased me all the more. Looking back I can see they weren't monsters—it seems to be normal behavior for kids to pick on those who are different. I don't think it did me any harm—it certainly stopped me from believing that the world revolved around my indulged little self! Nowadays if you want to hold your head up at dinner parties, an unhappy childhood is practically a necessity.''

''What were the circumstances that actually took you back to the King Country?'' he asked idly.

The chocolate in her mouth tasted suddenly of ashes. Mindful of her policy never to tell lies, always to stick to the truth even if it wasn't the whole truth, she said, ''My parents died, and I went to live with an aunt.''

''That was hard.''

She nodded. ''They left a gap,'' she said quietly, and began to talk of the Spoleto Festival held each year in Charleston, that magnificent city of elegant houses and tantalizing gardens on the mainland.

He followed suit, and by the time the coffee was served she'd decided that Nicholas Leigh was a perfect host. He had a bred-in-the-bone savoir faire that made the evening go smoothly, his conversation was interesting if a little uncompromising—he was not one to suffer fools gladly—and he had the rare attribute of charm, the ability to make the woman who was with him feel she was the only person who mattered to him.

Which, considering the career he'd chosen, had to come in very handy.

And she shouldn't be here with him—for so many reasons she couldn't even pick out the most important.

''What's the matter?''

Add intelligent and perceptive to that list of endowments, she thought sardonically. ''Nothing. I'm sorry, I really am a little tired.''

His swift glance might have indicated disbelief, but he asked merely, ''Where are you off to next?''

She said, ''France for five days.''

''Paris?''

''Yes,'' she said, wondering exactly what emotion tinged his deep tones.

''With a man?''

Cool, opaque as turquoise, her eyes met his without flinching. "And his secretary."

Although she sensed a tightly leashed speculation beneath the impassive features, he said aloofly, "Where do you go from there?"

"Some heavy-duty interpreting in Kuala Lumpur."

"Ah, yes, the ASEAN conference."

"Well, I won't actually be at the conference. I'll be working for a company that sees good pickings there." She forestalled his next inquiry by saying with deliberate insouciance, "Then I have two weeks in New York, after which I'm taking three whole days off to paint my apartment."

He nodded, the movement of his head catching the glow from the candles so that his hair gleamed with bronze highlights. "You certainly get around. Is this peripatetic life the reason you haven't married?"

"One of them."

"And the others?"

Hiding her unease with flippancy, she parried, "The same reasons you haven't married, probably."

"Have you had a lover?"

The question was so unexpected she gave him the answer before she had time to restrain herself. Not in words, but it might as well have been; her eyes widened as they were captured by the golden flames that had entirely engulfed the green in his.

"Yes," he murmured, his smile narrow and sharp as a blade, "of course you have."

"You already knew it," she said, the hairs on the back of her neck lifting in a primitive, involuntary response to an unspoken threat. "It must have turned up on my security clearance."

"It did." His gaze held hers, glittering, mesmerizing. "I even know the man. Diplomatic circles are small, and we've met several times. What possessed you to fall in love with a

British diplomat, Mariel, and then dump him with his self-esteem shattered?''

Oh, David...

Something—fear?—twisted deep inside her, but she said evenly, "My personal life—"

"Your personal life is inextricably bound up with your professional life," he said, watching her. "As you well know. Just as mine is. Apart from your facility for languages, the most important thing you have to offer is your reliability, and the fact that you can be trusted not to let out secrets."

Racked by outrage and fear, she angled her chin at him. "I don't," she said. "As you say, if I did, my career would be down the drain."

"Why did you dump David St. Clair, Mariel?"

"It's none of your business," she said stiffly. "It was entirely personal." Like so much she had told this man it was only a half-truth. Each word was like a marble on her tongue, heavy and hard to manage, but she thought she produced the right offended snap.

"Unfortunately," he said with a grim inflection that sent a shiver the length of her spine, "I'm fighting an urge to make it my business. Let's get out of here."

Ignoring her protests, he again insisted on accompanying her to the staff quarters. Once outside, she said with gritty restraint, "At times your mother's rules must make your life uncomfortable."

"I've always thought that was a mother's function in life," he returned, the flash of anger gone as though it had never emerged.

"Rule by guilt?" It didn't sound like the dictum of a woman who had lived openly as a married man's mistress.

"My mother didn't go in for guilt. Discomfort is different. She was very good at discomfort." He spoke with a kind of sardonic tolerance, as though in spite of mixed feelings for his mother, he'd been fond of her.

"It doesn't seem to have done you any harm." A hint of acid etched the words.

"I'm sure it didn't. I was a reasonably normal boy, which means I had all the sensitivity of a concrete path." He pushed aside the branch of an old crepe myrtle, holding it back so that it wouldn't snag her hair.

And she didn't believe that, either. He was far too perceptive to be self-centered. Abruptly, because she was afraid he might begin to talk about her family, she changed the subject. "How do you think this miniconference is going?"

"So far, so good."

Well, discretion was part of his job. Still raw from his questions over dinner, she disregarded caution and probed more deeply. "Do you think the discovery that both Mr. McCabe and Mr. Watanabe are swordsmen has been a breakthrough?"

"It's certainly given them something to talk about," he said sardonically, "as well as adding to your vocabulary."

"I understand trade comes up tomorrow as a subject for discussion."

"Does it?"

"Apparently. Mr. McCabe made some joke about having to read papers tonight as his memory is so bad, and both he and Mr. Watanabe vied with each other to establish how generally useless they are as ministers." When he said nothing she went on, "I suppose you'll be on duty." More silence, which she felt compelled to fill. "You did say your specialty was trade, didn't you?"

"I did."

They came to a bend in the path, shaded by a magnolia draped in fairy lights that sparkled like earthbound stars amongst the sculptured foliage. A soft, magical light silvered the pale trunk and branches, yet the very glimmer caused the surrounding shadows to press closely about them in the cool, sea-scented air.

"I've been wondering about you, Mariel," he said quietly.

That unsettling, stupid fear uncurled in the pit of her stomach. "I can't imagine why," she said with a brisk, no-nonsense intonation. "I'm very ordinary."

"Helen of Troy probably thought she was very ordinary." He paused, then went on harshly, "I've been wondering why the way your top lip curls when you smile drives me mad. And why the sound of your voice has the same effect on me as fur on bare skin. And why your eyes go smoky when you say my name, and exactly what the secrets are that lie hidden in their depths..."

He spoke the last few words against her lashes. His arms pulled her closer, and his mouth crushed hers as his voice echoed eternally in the furthermost reaches of her soul, stealing away her wits and her willpower in a flood of blazing eroticism.

She had waited for this for years, Mariel thought dazedly, head flung back, arms curling around his shoulders. All her life. She had been born for him. Making love to David had been joyous and satisfying, but Nicholas fired her blood with an uncivilized, wholly elemental hunger that ate through her self-possession, a white-hot intensity of sensation roaring through her body with the force and purpose of a volcanic explosion.

How could one man do this to her?

And what the hell was she getting into?

Terrified by the ferocity of her response, she tore her mouth free and pushed vainly against the cage of his arms, taking in great gulps of air, her hands pressed flat on his chest. The primitive rhythm of his heart drove violently into her palms. She looked up past the elegant black and white of his evening clothes, past the broad sweep of shoulder and chest into his strong-boned face.

Hooded, half-closed eyes scanned her face. To her shock she realized that the fierce pressure making her lips tingle had marked his, too; they were fuller, more sensual in the lean, ascetic features.

"I don't want this," she gasped when the torrent in her blood had eased slightly.

"Nobody could want that," he said, his voice deep and sensual and slightly rough. "It's like a tidal rip, deceptively smooth on the surface, but one step into it and it carries you off to drown. However, want it or not, it's there. What are we going to do about it?"

Was he asking whether she wanted an affair? At that moment, her body still shaking with the consuming desire he had roused, she wanted nothing more than to give in to the mindless need and let it take her over.

But she was more than just her body. And this man spelled danger, a spellbinding, sexual power that lured her on, enmeshing her in his primeval magnetism.

With eyes dilated by the night and its unexpected, imprudent passion, she searched his face for some sign of softness, of tenderness.

He was looking at her with a dispassionate interest that maddened her as much as it warned her. Although she'd been almost ambushed by need, he, in spite of his words, had not. If she surrendered to this rash, ill-judged hunger, he would take whatever she was prepared to give him, but he would still be in full control of himself and, ultimately, of her.

It was this that gave her the courage to quell the importunate demands of her body and mutter beneath her breath, "Nothing. I'm not doing anything about it. I don't go to bed with people I've only known a couple of days."

"How long had you known David St. Clair before you went to bed with him?"

Three months. David was a gentleman.

And Nicholas Leigh, for all his English tailoring and effortless air of authority, was not. Her first intuition had been correct; not quite hidden beneath the sophisticated urbanity lurked the prowling menace of a hunter, lethal and cold-bloodedly intimidating.

She said in a hard voice, "That's none of your business."

"What happened, Mariel?" he asked without emphasis, as though they had not just shared a kiss, as though the foundations of her world had not trembled and almost collapsed.

She said remotely, "We agreed that we wouldn't be happy together."

I told him about my past and he decided that it made me—as a wife, as a mistress, as a lover—a distinct handicap to any ambitious diplomat. And you would make exactly the same decision.

"Why do you want to know?" she continued, using anger and scorn to disassociate herself from the woman of only a few minutes ago who had shivered in his arms, pressed closer to his strong body, gloried in his swift, primal response.

"Curiosity, perhaps. Did you love him?"

Because she wanted to shake that imperturbable composure she told him the truth, hissing between her teeth, "Yes, I loved him."

"For a while." Nicholas spoke calmly, yet his eyes were fixed on her face with a keen interest, as though she were some exotic creature he planned to dissect.

She took a deep breath and moved away, running shaking hands through her hair, freeing the damp strands on her temple and at the nape of her neck. Although her pulse had evened out, his nearness was still intensely disturbing.

"Your questions are incredibly rude," she said curtly. "I need to get some sleep."

He must have realized he had pushed her far enough, for he responded, "Let's go, then."

They were almost at the staff quarters when they heard an eerie little noise that emanated from a hidden garden not far from the path.

"Someone's crying," Mariel said, turning toward the sound.

"Stay there."

She shook her head. "It sounds like a—"

"Stay there." He set off toward the mysterious weeper.

Mariel hesitated for only a few seconds before following him the length of the smoothly clipped hedge of azaleas to the single opening. Inside, a sweep of smooth grass surrounded a circular bed of white azaleas, incandescent in the moonlight, as was the marble statue of a nymph at their center.

Huddled amongst the low bushes was a child, her face swollen and blotchy as she wept forlornly into her hands.

"Caitlin," Mariel exclaimed, running over to her. "What are you doing out here?"

Nicholas dropped onto his knee beside her. "It can't be that bad," he said, his deep voice amazingly gentle. "Your little face is all swollen—is that tears or mosquitoes?"

Caitlin sobbed, "I want my mommy."

"Then let's go and find her," Nicholas said.

"I'm not allowed," she wailed, and sobbed more loudly.

There was a hopeless, lost quality about the sound that tore at Mariel's heart. "Darling, Mommy might be cross with you for running away, but she loves you very much. Come on, we'll take you home."

"No, I have to stay." Her gulping sobs sent Mariel fishing for a handkerchief.

"Here," Nicholas said, thrusting an unfolded one into her hand.

Tipping the small, drenched face, Mariel blotted the tears, saying in what she hoped was the right maternal tone, "Come on, blow your nose. You'll feel a lot better if you do."

Obediently the child did that, before saying in a voice thickened with tears, "I w-want my mommy, *now!*"

"I know you do," Mariel said, "so why do you have to stay here?"

Caitlin folded her lips, holding back the words, but guilt and fear and indecision were written large in her features.

Nicholas said, "Come on, then, Caitlin, we'll take you back to the quarters—"

"No—" she cried, breaking into tears again. "I'm not allowed, I'm not allowed . . ."

Making soothing noises, Mariel rocked the chubby little form against her shoulder until the panic-stricken weeping died away into choked hiccuping sounds.

Nicholas bent over her, easing a strand of wet hair back from her forehead. "Why do you have to stay here?" he asked without emphasis.

Sniffing, Caitlin burrowed into Mariel's chest. "I'm not allowed to tell," she whimpered.

"Is Daddy coming?" Mariel asked softly.

After a long hesitation the rumpled head moved up and down against her breasts. Nicholas stood up. Uneasily conscious of his searching look around the garden, Mariel said, "We'll have to go back, darling. He must have meant you to wait for him at the compound."

"No, he said under the pretty lady. We had a picnic here when he came to see me, and he said to wait for him here."

Definitely worried now, Mariel released Caitlin and stood up, holding out her hand. "We need to get back to the compound," she said to Nicholas, speaking softly.

"I think I get the idea. I'll take her."

"He's probably around . . ."

"Keep your eyes open." Nicholas leaned down. "There's ice cream waiting for you," he coaxed, unerringly homing in on every child's greatest weakness. "Would you like some?"

Wide-eyed, Caitlin nodded.

"I'll give you a ride if you like," he offered.

Clearly wavering, the child glanced at him doubtfully, then nodded and silently held up her arms. He swung her up, cuddled her into his shoulder and said, "Right, let's go."

They were back on the path to the staff quarters when he suddenly stopped and handed the child to Mariel. "Get her out of here," he commanded beneath his breath as he turned toward a large live oak.

Mariel had never seen Elise's ex-husband, but she recognized him as he walked out from the shade of the big tree; in spite of his thickset, muscular body, he bore a striking resemblance to the child struggling in her arms. Against him Nicholas looked almost slender, his natural grace overshadowed by the brute physical power of the other man.

"Put her down," he ordered.

Crying, "Daddy!" Caitlin almost jumped out of Mariel's arms.

Silently fighting the wriggling, sobbing child, Mariel tightened her grip and walked down the path toward the compound. She could see the lights now quite clearly, but she was beginning to wonder whether she'd be able to get Caitlin there before her arms gave way.

Jimmy Jennings snapped, "Let her go!"

"She's not going to," Nicholas said crisply. "This is no way to go about things, man!"

"You keep your nose out of my business." His voice became harsher. "I said, lady, for you to put her down."

Setting her teeth, Mariel kept on walking. Caitlin wasn't a big child, but she was resisting every step of the way, and in spite of the adrenaline flooding her system, Mariel wasn't sure she had enough strength to make it before Jimmy lost patience. Of course he'd have to deal with Nicholas, who was walking between her and Jimmy. She stole a quick look at the two men. Oh, God, Jimmy was huge, his fists clenching and unclenching, his bulk ominous in the dappled light. If he hit Nicholas he could hurt him severely.

Yet she couldn't let Caitlin go.

"She's my kid," Jimmy said angrily, keeping pace. "You want to live with me, don't you, honey? We can go to Disneyland—"

Nicholas broke into Caitlin's wail. "You don't have custody so you'd be kidnapping her, and that's a serious offense that'll put you in jail for more years than you can count."

"Got to catch us first," Jimmy boasted. "I'm not as stupid as some people think—I know what to do. Anyway, her momma goes out to work all day, only sees her at night. That's no way—"

Mariel said coldly, "If you'd given her enough to live on, instead of declaring bankruptcy—"

"Shut up," Nicholas interrupted brusquely at the same time as Caitlin's father spoke.

"She left me," he said, his voice rising. "Now you listen, and you do just what I tell you to, lady, because I've got a gun."

Horrified, Mariel spared him another swift glance. Sure enough, something gleamed evilly in Jimmy's hand. Sudden, abject fear robbed her limbs of strength. She staggered, but clutched her burden more tightly and managed to regain her footing. Swiftly Nicholas moved across to support her with a strong hand, still positioning himself between her and the man who threatened them.

Nicholas, she thought, striving to suppress her panic, Nicholas, be careful!

Angry, baffled frustration roughened Jimmy's voice. "You put her down nice and slow on the ground, lady. Nice and easy. She's precious, and I don't want anyone to hurt her."

"What sort of life is she going to have while you're on the run?" Nicholas said, his hand in the small of Mariel's back, propelling her on when she instinctively slowed. He continued without a pause, speaking almost conversationally.

"You'll have to go into hiding, which means you'll never be able to send her to school, so she'll grow up illiterate. You won't be able to make close friends in case you give yourself away, so she won't know how to behave in company. And although she wants to go with you now, she's going to miss her mother and pine for her as much as she's pined for you. Is that what you want for her? Unhappiness and bitterness? Because she's old enough to know what you've done, and how do you think she'll feel about you in ten years' time when she realizes just what she's missed because of you?"

"She won't miss anything," Jimmy said angrily. "I'll look after her properly—she's my baby, as well as that bitch's. I'm not going to hurt her!"

He seemed to be trying to justify himself. Mariel saw moonlight gleam on a wildly waving gun, and she swallowed. But she understood Nicholas's tactics and, in spite of quivering legs and arms and a dry throat, in spite of fear that clutched her stomach and numbed her brain, she kept walking toward the compound. Caitlin stopped struggling and turned her face toward her father, her brow furrowed. Praying she'd stay that way, Mariel wished Nicholas would get out of the line of fire.

She didn't like the hint of desperation in Jimmy's voice. She was safe—he wouldn't try to shoot her while she carried Caitlin—but Nicholas was not. If Jimmy lost his head...

Nicholas's strong hand slid around her waist and forced her relentlessly on as he said evenly, "What about college? If you're on the run you're not going to be able to save enough money to send her to college. Is that what you want for her? A dead-end job slinging hash in some roadside café? That's if she gets enough education to be able to qualify for college."

"I've got money," Jimmy said harshly. "I tell you, I love her! I've thought this all out—she'll be happier with me than with her mother...."

The walls of the converted stables loomed closer. Another twenty-five yards—surely she could hang on for another twenty-five yards.

Fear tasted metallic in her mouth. Thank God Caitlin was quiescent. Still staring at her father, she was clinging to Mariel.

"You just leave that to me to work out," Jimmy snarled, suddenly losing patience. "Lady, if you don't put her down right now, I'm going to shoot your man. And I'm a good shot, so I'll get him. After all, if I've got to go to jail for kidnapping, it's not going to make much difference if there's a murder charge on the indictment, too."

"I don't care how good a shot you are," Nicholas said calmly. "You're quite likely to miss. Handguns are not accurate enough for you to be certain you'll hit me. How would you feel if the bullet found another mark—someone small?"

"You get away from them," Jimmy ordered fiercely.

Nicholas said, "No."

"Damn you, I can take you, anyway, without this." He spat the words as he came toward them in a rush, low and fast, his arms spread wide.

Another surge of adrenaline boosted Mariel, but it was Nicholas's swift push that got her to Elisa's door.

Caitlin began to cry again, wailing, "Daddy, Daddy, Daddy..."

A door jerked backward, and Elise stood there, wild-eyed and panic-stricken. "Oh, God," she cried, rushing forward and grabbing her daughter from Mariel's arms. Caitlin's crying soared into a crescendo.

"Get inside," Mariel hissed, pushing mother and child toward Elise's door.

She turned just in time to see Nicholas deliver a swift, sharp chop somewhere in the region of Jimmy's throat. The other man let out an inhuman grunt as he dropped, then lay motionless on the ground.

"Oh!" She raced across the grass. "Are you all right?" she demanded urgently.

Nicholas didn't even seem to be breathing more heavily than normal, although his eyes glittered, and when she got closer she could see a faint sheen of sweat on his forehead.

"I'm fine." He dropped on his knee beside the unconscious Jimmy and touched the pulse in his neck. "So is he, although he's not going to feel too good when he wakes up."

"Is that a gun?" Elise's horrified voice came from behind them.

Mariel looked up, but Elise was alone.

"It's all right," she said, "she's with Saranne." Her breath caught. She looked down at the man who had been her husband and asked sickly, "What did he do?"

As Nicholas checked the pistol, Mariel told her in a few concise sentences exactly what had happened.

By the time she'd finished, Jimmy was beginning to stir. Elise looked down at him with hard eyes. "So that's what it was all about. I suppose he somehow got a message to Caitlin."

The man on the ground moaned. Elise said bitterly, "I could kill him! He's put her through hell."

Nicholas straightened. "For what it's worth," he said mildly, "he didn't sound as though he meant her any harm. Or anyone—there're no bullets in this thing."

"Oh, that's just so typical! Of course he wouldn't hurt her—he loves her—but he's such a fool," Elise said angrily. "He's never grown up. He thinks if he wants something he should have it, and I don't think he's ever going to get past it. He's a clever man—he's made a lot of money, worked himself out of the village here and into his own business—but he's just a spoiled kid at heart."

"Do you want to lay a charge?" Nicholas asked neutrally.

Elise stared at him. "Do you?" she asked.

Nicholas said, "Not particularly. I can understand how he feels, although I don't condone his behavior. But it occurs to me that a good lawyer should be able to use this incident to everyone's advantage—even, perhaps, your ex-husband's."

"NICHOLAS WAS just wonderful," Elise enthused the next morning. "After you left us we had a long talk—he's very easy to talk to, isn't he?—and then he suggested some ways of stopping Jimmy's harassment. He's clever. He more or less manhandled Jimmy to his cousin's down in the village. I've just been talking to my lawyer, and he thinks that we've got enough on Jimmy to get a much better deal than the one we got originally. He's contacting Jimmy's lawyer."

"I'm so glad," Mariel said.

Elise looked at her. "Jimmy wouldn't have shot you or Nicholas," she said earnestly. "He thinks he's a hard man, but he's not violent. Still, you weren't to know that, or that the gun wasn't loaded. Nicholas said you kept your head and just went on walking. I can't thank you enough."

Mariel said bracingly, "I knew I was quite safe while I had Caitlin."

But Elise's eyes filled with tears. "Most people panic when someone waves a gun at them, but Nicholas said you didn't. You and Nicholas saved her. I'm never going to forget that."

"How is she now?"

Elise swallowed and blew her nose. "Oddly enough, she seems all right. I suppose part of this was my fault. I should have let him see her, but I was so mad when he declared bankruptcy I got as obstructive as possible, and I said he couldn't call her anymore. He's been calling her at his cousin's. Saranne knew, but she didn't tell me, because she thought I was being unreasonable.''

"That seems a little remiss of her," Mariel said caustically.

Elise shrugged. "She's known Jimmy all her life. She never thought he'd pull a stunt like this. Well, neither did I. What happened last night shocked us all."

"Me, too," Mariel said fervently. "Is Caitlin at school today?"

"Yes. I thought it better to behave as though everything was normal. I think she's relieved she doesn't have to go with Jimmy. She keeps asking when we're going to see him, and I've promised that they can have time together. At least I've got some hold on him now. I told my lawyer exactly what happened, and I'm going to write it out and sign it and give it to him to keep, and if Jimmy puts one foot out of line, I'll take him to court. After that, well, we'll just have to wait and see. He might have learned a lesson."

Mariel certainly hoped so; her blood still ran cold at the memory of the gun wavering in Jimmy's hand, and Nicholas walking between her and it.

CHAPTER FIVE

DURING THE FOLLOWING exhausting two days Mariel avoided Nicholas as much as she could. Apparently the discovery of the ministers' shared interest in swordplay had ended the preliminaries, because both delegations settled down to hard work. Nicholas was always there, an obviously valued aide to Mr. McCabe, but he made no attempt to seek Mariel out, for which she was profoundly grateful.

Common sense warned her that she'd only cause herself grief if she allowed her heart any latitude beyond a casual interest in a virile, attractive and dominant man.

So she did her best to keep her mind firmly on her job and managed reasonably well, although her sleep was still haunted by dreams.

By the time it was over and the talks had wound up amidst goodwill all around, she was living on the ragged edge of her nerves. After the Japanese deputation had flown out on the afternoon helicopter, she changed into amber-colored silk trousers and a long silk top and went into the bar to say goodbye to Desmond.

"Mineral water?" he asked, automatically reaching for the small green bottle.

She grinned. "No, I think I'll have some champagne," she said.

Desmond lifted his brows.

"It's all right," Mariel said confidentially. "I only ever have one."

"I didn't think you drank."

"I don't when I'm working."

He poured a glass of champagne, saying, "I hear the Japanese have gone. The New Zealanders are leaving tomorrow morning?"

As she nodded his gaze moved to focus just behind and above her head. The skin on the back of her neck tightened, raising tiny hairs in an atavistic reaction to danger. She hadn't heard a sound, but even without Desmond's reaction she'd have known who'd just arrived.

"Good evening, sir," Desmond said smoothly. "Whiskey and soda?"

"Thank you." Nicholas's voice was even, but she thought she heard a note of disapproval in it.

Deliberately she lifted the glass of champagne to her lips. It was utterly ridiculous to feel guilty.

Ridiculous or not, she took only the smallest of sips before turning her head so that she could see the man behind her.

It was a small, treacherous blow to her pride to realize he wasn't looking at her. His eyes were fixed on Susan Waterhouse, standing with a couple of the younger New Zealanders on the other side of the room, and he was frowning.

I am not in the least jealous, Mariel told herself firmly.

"Come with me," Nicholas said, his voice breaking into her scattered, tumbling thoughts. His glance commanded, but that wasn't what pulled her to her feet.

Perhaps the champagne wasn't a good idea. When he looked at her like that, all pure male charisma backed by a hard, confident authority, she'd follow him across the world, an unwanted response that had to be caused by the bubbles in her blood.

Then again, the champagne might have nothing to do with it at all; it could be simply her response to the savage compulsion that stirred in her every time she saw him.

"Where are we going?"

"I said I'd join the others."

She most emphatically did not want to head across the room, but she did. She concentrated on being good company, even though it was difficult with Peter Sanderson's avid glance flicking from the cool, patrician beauty of Susan Waterhouse's face to Nicholas's, across to meet Mariel's bland gaze, and then back again, a tiny spark of malice lurking in his eyes.

Within minutes she discovered who that malice was directed at.

When someone mentioned the excellent examples of art in the hotel, he said, "They've even got a Picasso, Susan. One of his blue period. I noticed it specially because you and Nicholas had a signed print very like it in your flat in London. Remember? It hung in the sitting room over a rather nice inlaid sort of cabinet."

In the long, wakeful nights, Mariel had wondered what exactly her feelings were for Nicholas. She discovered now that she was fiercely, angrily, outrageously jealous of the woman with whom he'd lived. She sipped more champagne, keeping an iron hold on her features because Peter Sanderson was watching her with a gleeful smugness. Why had he deliberately dropped that piece of gossip into the conversation? What reaction had he hoped for?

And exactly what was the relationship between Susan and Nicholas now?

"It turned out to be a fake," Susan said regretfully, "so Nicholas made them take it back."

Peter Sanderson's laugh had an artificial note in it. "I thought you liked it."

"I did, but I have an objection to being sold something as genuine when it's not," Nicholas said.

Mariel looked down into the pale golden liquid in her glass. In the back of her brain she knew that the bubbles kept on rising, that there was noise and laughter in the bar, that the conversation around her continued, but all she could think of was that Susan Waterhouse and Nicholas had been lovers who had shared a flat and bought pictures together and decided where to hang them.

It hurt damnably. She felt as though he'd betrayed her, and telling herself that she was reacting with utter stupidity didn't help.

She meant to excuse herself, but somehow found herself having dinner in the restaurant with Mr. McCabe, Susan and Nicholas, as well as the two older women in the delegation. No one peered strangely at her or asked her if she felt all right, so she supposed she behaved normally.

What both unsettled and pained her was Susan's air of calm possessiveness where Nicholas was concerned. Not that the other woman was making a point; she merely treated him with the intimate friendliness of those who know each other extremely well. In spite of her severest admonitions, Mariel felt herself prickling like an angry cat. It didn't help that Nicholas showed no signs of reciprocating. He didn't differentiate between Susan and the others of the party or— and this was the rub—between Susan and Mariel.

Profoundly grateful when the dinner finally finished, Mariel still had more torment to endure. The trade minister decided he wanted her to check over just one last paper, so she and Nicholas went up to his suite six doors down from Nicholas's, and she spent two hours drafting the translation of a working document. Officially, of course, she was off duty, but it didn't occur to her to refuse.

When at last it was over and she was able to go, Nicholas walked down the corridor with her.

"How is the child?" he asked. "Caitlin?"

She sighed. "She seems to be all right. Elise has found a therapist who specializes in children. She hopes they'll be able to straighten out any residual problems."

"What's she decided to do about the husband?"

"He's agreed to give her a much bigger share of the assets he'd squirreled away before going bankrupt, so things will be easier financially for her. In return, Elise has agreed to let him have supervised access to Caitlin. She doesn't think he'll ever realize what he was doing to the child, but she did admit that her stubbornness made things worse. Anyway, they have some hope of working things out so Caitlin isn't being torn apart. Elise is very grateful for all your help. Caitlin calls you the nice man who talks funny."

He smiled. It would have been foolish to say his face softened, but for a moment Mariel thought she could see how he'd look when he gazed at his own children. "I like children. Most children, anyway."

"You certainly handled her well. Do you have any of your own?"

He sent her an ironic sideways glance. "No, I've never been married."

"They don't necessarily go together," she said in her driest tone.

He said directly, "For me they do. I'm conventional in my outlook. I don't intend to have children until I marry."

She didn't mean to say it—she didn't stand on such terms with him—yet the words came too swiftly to call them back. "Perhaps Susan?"

"We lived together for a few months," he said, his voice deep and emotionless and hard. "It's been over for a year now."

Mariel found such cool dispassion repellent. Very crisply she demanded, "What happened?"

"I don't feel it's any of your business," he returned caustically, firing her own words back at her.

Embarrassed more by her own boldness than his snub, she flushed and muttered, "No, of course not."

She hadn't really been prying. Somehow she had the strange feeling that she could discuss anything with Nicholas; it hurt and shamed her that he should find her interest prurient.

Perhaps that was how he'd felt when he'd asked her about David.

They had been walking slowly and were almost abreast of his door. He said savagely, "Oh, damn, I didn't mean that the—"

Footsteps sounded along the corridor. Someone laughed. It had all the hallmarks of an old bedroom farce, especially when Nicholas muttered a short, succinct curse under his breath, opened the door into his room, took her by the wrist and pulled her in with him, slamming the door behind her.

"Bloody Sanderson," he said with barely leashed anger as he released her.

For some reason she shivered.

"What's the matter?"

Relapsing into schoolgirl vernacular she said, "He gives me the creeps."

"Why?" he demanded sharply. "What's he done?"

"Nothing." Shocked by the darkness in his tone, his expression, she shook her head. "Nothing at all—I've barely exchanged words with him. He just seems very intense, even a bit unbalanced. Especially," she added deliberately, "where you're concerned."

Nicholas crossed to the tray on the sideboard and said, "You look as though you need a drink."

"No, thanks." She hesitated, then went on rapidly before she could change her mind, "I didn't mean to pry about your relationship with Susan. No, that's not right, I did, but . . . I'm sorry, it's absolutely no business of mine."

"And I," he said on a jagged note of self-derision, "understand your curiosity. After all, I share it. That's why I asked those impertinent questions about St. Clair. I assume it's another manifestation of this highly inconvenient attraction." He bent and peered into the refrigerator, standing up to say, "There's lemonade here."

She said, "Well, in that case, thanks."

He brought her some, and for a moment she sat holding the rapidly frosting glass. She shouldn't be here, she thought.

"We were thinking of marriage," he said, "but in the end we decided not."

Why? A glance at his face told Mariel she wasn't going to find that out, and she didn't want to hear any more. The thought of Nicholas planning to marry anyone sent a wave of panicky outrage through her.

You're getting in too deep, she told herself, and asked the first thing that came to mind. "Why does Peter Sanderson hate you so much?"

"Because I was born rich and he was born poor."

"Oh, come on, now," she protested. "In New Zealand that doesn't matter. I mean, he's in the diplomatic service and so are you!"

"Money matters everywhere in the world," he said cynically. "However, he has a little more than that to base his dislike on. I got a posting he wanted, and because he can't believe it was any deficiency of his that lost it for him, he prefers to think I called on the old school-tie network to ease my path."

"I see." Lemonade trickled cold and sweet over her tongue. She swallowed and said, "I think he could be dangerous. He sounded almost driven."

Nicholas's glance, keen and sudden as a falcon's heart-dropping swoop from the sky, chilled her. "Possibly. However, I'm not afraid of him."

No, he wouldn't be. Tartly she snapped, "I don't suppose you're afraid of anything!"

He certainly hadn't been afraid of Jimmy, gun or no gun. He had used his astute, diplomatic brain to unsettle the other man, kept him neatly off balance, and then, when force was needed, used it with cool, ruthless efficiency.

"Then you're wrong," he said calmly. "Only an idiot doesn't have fears."

She took another tiny sip of lemonade and asked with
what she hoped sounded like idle curiosity, "What fright-
ens you?"

He gave her an enigmatic, not unamused, smile. "Losing control," he admitted.

"So you're a control freak. Somehow I'm not surprised." Her voice was light, all traces of speculation hidden.

"What are *you* afraid of?"

"Fair trades?" Turning her mouth down at the corners in
a grimace, she started to return a flippant answer. And then
she thought, no, he told you the truth.

"Rejection," she said quickly, surprising herself.

Until the moment the word fell into the silence between
them, she hadn't known exactly what she feared, and now
that she had said it she felt the power of it right through to
her marrow.

"Because your parents died, I suppose," Nicholas said,
astounding her. "To a child that must seem like the ultimate rejection."

Afraid she had revealed far too much, she sent him a
brittle, resentful glance. "Pop psychology?" she asked
tauntingly.

"More like common sense to me." He sounded relaxed,
almost sympathetic, as though he understood her fierce denial of his insight.

She put down the glass of lemonade. The one glass of
champagne she'd drunk before dinner couldn't be the cause
of the bewitching, treacherous siren's song singing through
her veins. The big room with its elegant furnishings was
alien, unnerving. Her eyes slid over the end posts of the bed,
picking out carved ears of rice. A sudden heat coursed
through her body.

"I'd better go," she said carefully, getting to her feet.

His green-gold gaze mocked her, but he stood, too, and
said, "Yes, I suppose you should."

He opened the door, walking down the corridor beside her. This time they had it completely to themselves, although muted noise from the bar indicated that plenty was happening there. A long night for Desmond, she thought.

Silently they walked down the brick pathway beneath the majestic live oaks and ancient crepe myrtles and huge, flowering camellias that looked to be as old as the hotel building itself, breathing in cool air scented with the faint perfume of azaleas.

This would be the last time she saw him, Mariel thought, oppressed by a nameless, painful emotion.

"I'm going to walk on the beach," Nicholas said. "Coming?"

Mariel knew she should say no. "All right," she said.

He turned and struck across the grass, skirting the trees and unerringly leading them to the beach.

"Do you navigate by the stars?" she asked flippantly.

"Like migrating birds, all the way from Cape Reinga to Siberia, then back again in six months' time?" He sounded amused. "I have an excellent sense of direction."

Was there anything he couldn't do well? Images flashed into her brain: Nicholas on the golf course, shooting, moving with feral, athletic grace as he dispatched Jimmy, Nicholas turning her heart over with the potent consuming intensity of his kiss.

Sand scrunched beneath her feet. She stopped and took off her shoes, holding them while she looked about for a safe hiding place. Not that anyone would steal them; the beach was completely deserted.

"Here," Nicholas said, taking them from her and putting them beside his on the edge of the beach. "Under the third palmetto from the end. Don't forget."

"Look away," she said.

Obediently he turned his back and she pulled her nylon stockings down and stuffed them into one of her shoes. "All right," she said gruffly.

Casually he scooped her hand into his and walked away from the boardwalk that protected the fragile dunes, over the soft sand, not stopping until they reached the firm, tide-packed surface.

"Why don't you go back to New Zealand?" he asked, his tone as casual as the light clasp on her fingers.

She had to swallow before she could say, "I've never wanted to."

"Never?"

"No."

He was silent for a hundred yards or so. Then he said, "You must really hate the place."

For some reason she couldn't come out and say it. "I just never felt it was home," she murmured.

"Was your aunt unkind to you?"

Biting her lip, she sent him a swift sideways glance. Aqueous, silvery light outlined the autocratic lines of his angular profile, emphasized the strong planes of his cheeks and forehead.

"She didn't want me," she surprised herself by telling him, "and I can't blame her for that. It was difficult for us both."

"Is she still there?"

"She died while I was in Japan." Before he could ask any more questions she said, "How about you? Have you a big extended family?"

"A few cousins," he said. "Nobody close."

"So it seems we're both adrift in the world."

"Adrift?" His voice was cool and considering. "Is that how you think of yourself? Lost and alone?"

"No, of course not." She spoke hurriedly, aware that something seemed to be missing from her answer. Pretending to see a shell in the hard-packed sand, she bent so that he couldn't see her face. "Far from it," she said as she stood up, forcing a brisk, cheerful note into her tone. "I have friends, a career I really enjoy, a future and a home. It was just a term, a word."

"A Freudian slip," he observed obliquely.

"Freud's being discredited, didn't you know?"

He smiled. "So I understand. I think I'll reserve my judgment."

She was seized with an urge to find out as much as she could about him before he left the island and they never saw each other again. "What do you like most about your career?" she asked.

His broad shoulders moved slightly as though he found the question irksome, but he answered without hesitation. "I enjoy feeling that in some small way I'm making a difference in the world. And I must admit I like pitting my wits against what sometimes seem like impossible odds. I relish finding ways through problems."

"Has it lived up to your expectations?" she asked.

"I'm a little less idealistic than when I started," he said dryly.

"Where have you been posted?"

"Australia first, and then London."

Mariel thought she might never enjoy anything more in her life than breathing in the crisp salt air as she listened to Nicholas tell her about his time in Canberra, the capital territory of Australia. Through his eyes she saw the huge, sunburned country as he had experienced it—its size, its awe-inspiring beauty and variety, the laconic, tough determination of its citizens in the face of sometimes almost unbeatable odds.

By a natural progression the conversation moved to London. To her secret delight, Mariel discovered that they admired many of the same things about the grimy old city. After a vigorous discussion on the state of the theater there, they moved on to art. When Mariel stated that modern art left her cold, confessing that her spiritual home in New York was the Metropolitan Museum of Art, Nicholas laughed, but began to discuss the subject with references to the pictures she had gazed at with affronted bewilderment in the Tate Gallery in London and the Guggenheim Museum. He made them come alive for her, and as they walked down the wide, white beach empty of everything but their two figures beneath a nebulous moon, she thought dreamily that she didn't ever want this to end.

Of course it had to, and in the most foolish manner. Too busy looking at him to notice where she was going, she tripped and he caught her, his arms taut and corded as he set her back on her feet.

The breath was sucked from her lungs. As she felt the imprint of his lean, lithe body, an answering need fogged her brain with slow, sensuous magnetism.

She saw exactly when he realized what was happening to her; his eyes narrowed, glinting beneath the dark lashes, and somehow his body sprang to life, a male pulse running through it in answer to the feminine summons of hers. She smiled, and he said harshly, "Damn," and bent his head and kissed her.

If he hadn't done that she might have been able to keep her dignity and self-esteem intact, but the moment his mouth touched hers something buried in her burst into flames, hotter than fire, more intense than the savage blast of the storm, and she was lost, giving herself up to him and to the sensations only he seemed able to arouse.

The kiss was long and unhurried and deep. Under its ensorcellment she forgot that she couldn't afford such an indulgence, forgot that Nicholas spelled danger to her, forgot everything except the soaring delight caused by his mouth on hers, the swift, overwhelming response of her body.

But eventually he lifted his head and said in a thick, impeded voice, "No, this is impossible."

He didn't know how impossible it was. Yet she couldn't stop; she turned her head into his throat and with leisurely, delicate greed touched her tongue to the pulse throbbing there. He tasted of salt and musk and man, of Nicholas. And he stiffened, his body hardening beneath the tiny caress.

"I know," she said languidly. "Absolutely impossible."

He laughed beneath his breath, ragged, uneven laughter, and caught her face by the chin and said roughly, "So stop it, you provoking witch."

"Why?" Her lashes flickered, hiding her eyes, keeping at bay logic and common sense, the practical, pragmatic, responsible part of her that was screaming warnings somewhere in her brain. "You said it was impossible and I agreed with you...."

Even to herself the words sounded slurred, as though she wasn't really saying them, as though another woman, someone she'd never met, was speaking through her. It should have been frightening; Mariel realized that far from being afraid, she was exhilarated, because in spite of his words he was just as strongly affected as she was.

His eyes were gleaming with barely suppressed desire, and the straight mouth was fuller; oh, he was still in control, but she could see his struggle to stay that way.

Lifting her hand, she cupped his jaw, her palm sensitive to the rough silk texture of his skin, the pulse that jerked beneath it.

"It doesn't matter," she said softly. "We're never going to see each other after tonight."

"Is that what you're offering? A one-night stand?"

His quiet, almost conversational tone didn't hide the brutal reality of his words. Mariel realized just what she was doing, the inevitable end of such an exchange.

Heat scorched along her cheekbones. She kept her hand against his skin for a moment, then removed it slowly, pride refusing to allow her to reveal the shame that ate with stark precision through her heated emotions.

"No," she said on a sigh. "No, but I must admit I'm sorely tempted."

He gave a thin smile. "So am I," he said harshly. "You make me forget to be sensible. Come on, we'd better go back."

The sooner she got away from him the less likely he'd recognize the chill that seeped through her, an ugly devastation of humiliation.

Hastily turning, she saw with some dismay just how far they'd walked down the beach. It was going to take them at least half an hour before they got back to their shoes.

"Heavens, we're almost at the cottages," she said, trying hard to keep her voice cool and level.

To her intense relief he followed her change of subject, turning with her, walking a little distance away. "What cottages?"

"Oh, they belong to the hotel, but they're for people who want real privacy. The road we crossed to get to the beach follows the coast." She gestured to the wooded margins of land behind the low dunes. "It's about three hundred yards behind those trees. It goes right down to the tip of the island and ends up at an old lighthouse. The cottages are between the road and the beach before you get to the lighthouse." Her voice sounded fine; she fractionally increased the speed of her walk, hoping to get it over with as quickly as possible.

"Is the lighthouse no longer in service?" he asked. Apparently he, too, wanted to hasten their progress; his long legs matched her pace without hesitation.

"It's been retired for years. Nobody lives there now, and it's sad and rather desolate."

Lonely, too, although Liz Jermain, who lived in the guest cottage farthest from the hotel, seemed to enjoy the silent stretches of beach and woods. Wise woman, Mariel thought bleakly, wishing that a similar emptiness stretched between her and Nicholas.

"Hardly anyone walks along here," she said, stubbornly filling the uncomfortable silence. "The hotel subtly discourages anyone from going farther than the beach spa. Most people find enough area between the hotel and the beach spa to satisfy their craving for sand.''

He asked idly, "What are they like, these cottages?''

"I believe they're very luxurious—old Mrs. Jermain, the hotel owner and Liz's grandmother, got a brilliant architect in to design them. With the beach in front and a thick strip of woodland between them and the road they're the most secluded accommodations on the island.''

He smiled. "They sound a bit like a New Zealand bach.''

"Not very,'' she said dryly. "Once I went for a holiday with our neighbor and her husband to the west coast, and I remember their bach vividly—camp stretchers, washing up in a bowl, tatty, ragged old sofas and deck chairs that fell to bits every five minutes. I loved it, but these cottages are for people who can afford to pay for security and privacy and luxury.''

"Sometimes I hope nothing ever changes in New Zealand,'' he said quietly. "I suppose there must be other places in the world where if you go to the beach and see someone else, you go away and find another beach, and where the most dangerous wildlife is a crab, but I haven't found any yet.''

It was vital to keep talking; while they talked she didn't have to face the hard ball of misery that lay like a lump in her chest, blocking her throat, aching in every cell. "New Zealand's not paradise,'' she retorted crisply. "Oh, I don't imagine I'll ever see a more beautiful country, but there are ugly people there, just as there are in any other country.''

"To a sensitive child from a cosmopolitan family, a small farming community in the King Country would have come as a distinct shock,'' he said. "But did it ever occur to you that they simply didn't know how to deal with you? You must have seemed as exotic as a rare gazelle, and you said yourself that children the world over are notorious for picking on those who are different.''

She wondered whether this was his personal experience, whether he had been made to feel different because of his parents.

But that was something she'd never know, because she'd come too close to him now and been singed by the fire of his masculinity. It was safer to keep her distance. So she said remotely, "Yes, of course," and for the rest of the long walk down the beach kept the conversation firmly on innocuous things.

CHAPTER SIX

"DO YOU MIND giving this week up?" Carole's voice was urgent. "Yeah, yeah, I know you're planning to paint your apartment, but you're wanted back in South Carolina. That must be a very up-market little hotel—you were only there a month ago for some high-powered conference, weren't you? Well, this sounds like another one."

Mariel's first instinct was to refuse, but common sense, the hard practicality that had kept her going over the past four weeks, stopped her. One of the reasons she did so well in her career was that she wasn't picky; apart from avoiding work with diplomats where she could, she was prepared to go anywhere at any time. She couldn't jeopardize her good reputation by refusing to go back to Bride's Bay Resort.

Nevertheless, she swallowed before saying to her agent in as casual a voice as she could produce, "Don't tell me more politicians want to spend more taxpayers' money amongst the alligators on the world-famous golf course."

"I don't know who they are," Carole said calmly. "All I know is the hotel contacted us yesterday and asked for you by name. You'll be there a week."

The mixture of paranoia and hope was vanquished by logic. Of course this job would have nothing to do with Nicholas. "All right."

"It's all organized. Pick up the tickets at the airport—you leave at seven tomorrow morning."

As THE HOTEL LAUNCH surged across to the low bulk of the island, Mariel kept her expression carefully blank. Five weeks ago she'd been placidly contented; her life had been pleasant. Oh, there hadn't been any great highs, but there'd been no deep, deathly lows, either, until Nicholas had blazed into it like a meteor, destructive and brilliant and overwhelming. She knew now that nothing was ever going to be the same again.

Of course she'd get over this corrosive anguish. Tangible though her grief and loneliness might be, the feeling that half her soul had been wrenched away was just a romantic illusion. David's rejection had taught her that no one suffered like this forever; in time she'd be happy again.

That was not what worried her. More dangerously, Nicholas had released another woman in her, a wild, hungrily sexual woman who'd made a total fool of herself, offering her body for a one-night stand!

Previous experience had taught her that she was not the most sensual of women. David had been a gentle lover, carefully making sure she reached her greatest peak, and she had responded with affection and a warm delight that bore absolutely no resemblance to the wild storm of desire Nicholas evoked with the mere touch of his hand on her skin. Mariel didn't know—didn't want to know—the woman who had stepped so far over the boundaries of her prior existence that she'd been temporarily out of her mind.

The only thing that comforted her was that for long moments Nicholas had been as caught up in the power of the moment as she had. Knowing that she was able to batter his unwavering control and wreck his composure so utterly satisfied some bewildering inner compulsion.

So it was all the more humiliating that he'd been able to reimpose the curb of his willpower on his passion while she'd lost prudence and caution, lost every tenet by which she'd lived her life until then.

Stop it, she ordered her restless brain, turning her head away from the other passengers so that nobody could see her face. *Stop it this instant.*

The launch docked, but when she went up to the hotel minivan, the driver consulted his list and said, "Ms. Browning? Oh, yes, here you are. No, ma'am, your party is at one of the guest cottages. The cart will be along— Ah, here it comes."

As the golf cart moved her and her luggage along the road past the hotel, past the dunes and the gardens and the beach spa, Mariel began to relax. On the beach people faded and dwindled, until soon it was a wide expanse of white sand, smooth as confectioner's sugar, empty of everything but the stately procession of big brown pelicans searching for food just offshore. The woods moved toward the road, enveloping it, the soft growth of young pines on the borders as feathery as ferns and the stiffer, more formal patterns of palmetto fronds giving the scene a subtropical air.

Subtropical climate, too; it was amazing how much difference a month made to the temperature. She loosened the button at the throat of her shirt and wondered hopefully whether she'd be able to work without having to wear panty hose. It was a relief when the trees gathered closely enough around the road to shade it.

At home we'd call this bush, she thought, then frowned. Home? New Zealand had never been home to her. That was another thing Nicholas had done—reminded her too vividly of the country she'd turned her back on. For years she'd managed very nicely without ever thinking of the place and the pain it represented; now repressed memories kept popping up all the time, bringing back the emotions of those bewildering years.

Fate, she thought wryly, had certainly had it in for her when it decided to send her down here back in April, dragging up old confusion and shock, old recollections, until she was as raw and unsure as a child on her first day of school.

She didn't feel anything like love for Nicholas, and yet she ached for him, wove more of those explicit, hungry fantasies into her dreams and missed him unbearably. He'd bewitched her; the physical attraction that had enmeshed them both was too potent to last, but meanwhile it enveloped her in a miasma of desire that colored her days and nights with all the hues of passion.

And thinking about him was the easiest way to keep the obsession alive, she told herself crossly, turning her head to stare about her.

At intervals, narrow tracks, barely wide enough for a car, disappeared into the woods on the seaward side, although the houses they served weren't visible. Each cottage had been designed as a totally secluded hideaway for people whose most precious luxury was privacy.

At least she wouldn't be continually tripped up by memories as she would've been at the hotel. She presumed she'd be staying with the ultradiscreet married couple who looked after the cottages and their inhabitants.

The golf cart turned down another barely discernible track and plunged into the undergrowth. Almost immediately they came to a large, spiked iron gate in a high wall. The driver brought the cart to a halt and got out to say something into a speaker set into the wall beside the gate. He was back at the wheel when the gates swung open.

Looking behind, Mariel saw that they closed immediately. No doubt there were cameras around. She shivered, glad she didn't live such a life. She would hate to be so endangered that security cameras were a necessity.

The cottage itself was not large. A low affair of white-painted weatherboard with a tiled roof, it was backed by pines and live oaks. The garden appeared to be entirely natural, a beautiful and spontaneous arrangement of trees and shrubs, grassy areas and small hillocks. The magical sussuration of a tiny stream formed a soothing counterpoint to the slow movement of the breeze in the pines that separated the grounds from the beach. Not for here the glorious explosion of azaleas and camellias that surrounded the hotel; whoever had designed the garden had insisted on a landscape as close to the natural as possible, and the unknown designer had been right.

"Go on in, ma'am," the driver said. "I'll bring your bags."

Mariel walked up the steps and through the open front door into the hall. The house seemed empty, but she heard music coming from behind a door; after standing irresolutely for a moment, she went over to it and knocked. No one answered.

"Hello," she called out. "Anybody home?"

And held her breath as she waited for an answer. It didn't come, so feeling oddly like Goldilocks, she opened the door and went through. She entered a big room furnished with the casual elegance of a summer cottage; glass doors folded back onto a deck. The music seemed to come from there. Cautiously she walked out into the sunlight.

The view took her breath away. In front of her was the garden and a pool, treated with such skill that for a moment she wondered whether it was a natural feature of the landscape. Beyond it a boardwalk led through pines and coastal scrub and palmettos to low dunes that formed a barrier between the house and the beach. The sea beckoned in an arc of soft blue under a hazy, cerulean sky.

The impact of such beauty ached in her heart, yet suddenly in her mind's eye she glimpsed an image of a golden sun set in a brilliant sky and breathed air so clear it tasted crystalline on the tongue. *New Zealand, get out of my brain*, she commanded, walking out into the sun.

A glorious soprano voice, smooth and perfect, sang words in a language Mariel thought she'd forgotten, left behind long years ago. It took only a spellbound moment before the significance of the music struck her with the force of a blow. The soprano was a New Zealand opera singer, and the song was a Maori one, loved and learned by generations of New Zealanders, a song of unrequited love.

She understood then, the image and the song, understood what she was doing there and why. But even as she turned to blunder back through the house, Nicholas said, "Mariel," and his hand caught her wrist, and she was looking up into eyes that gleamed with brilliant, blazing promise, at once a heart-stopping threat and a seduction.

"You're as white as a sheet," he said deeply, raising her hand to kiss first the fine bones of her wrist where the veins throbbed blue, and then the warm palm, his mouth a charm that robbed her both of strength and the travesty of peace she had worked so desperately to attain.

"You swine," she breathed above the thudding of her heart.

"For setting this up?" He laughed beneath his breath, his eyes hard yet satisfied as they scanned her face. "Would you have come if I'd asked you?"

"No. God, *no!*"

"I know."

Yanking her hand away, she clenched it to the overheated flurry of her heart as she glanced around the idyllic scene. Her brain felt as though someone had drowned her in wet concrete. She shook her head, trying to clear it, but when at last she managed to speak, the words came out as though she was afraid, instead of blindingly, savagely furious. "What's this all about?"

"It's the closest I could come to paradise on this side of the world." The straight line of his mouth twisted in self-derision. "For the first time in my life I'm being sentimental. It's embarrassing, but I find I can't be sensible where you're concerned."

Sensible! It seemed such an extraordinary word to use that she broke into laughter and had to physically quench it by clamping a hand over her mouth.

He said wryly, "I like it when you laugh. It reminds me that when the world looks like it's going to hell in a big way, there are still people who can be happy."

If only you knew, she thought, dragging her gaze from his face to stare around because she was too vulnerable to his potent male charisma. Although she thought she knew why he'd summoned her, she asked, "What am I doing here, Nicholas?"

"Having a holiday," he said promptly.

"I can't afford a holiday."

"You told me you were going to take this week off to paint your apartment. And I've covered it financially with your agency—they'll get their fee."

Somehow that made it seem as though he was paying for her time. Her swift, scorching look clashed with eyes that were altogether too perceptive.

"You know that's not it," he said crisply. "I thought you'd enjoy a holiday, Mariel, and because I organized this, I need to be sure you won't lose financially."

It made sense. The agency would certainly expect its cut of her supposed wages for the week. Wavering, fighting a strange little sense of disillusion, she asked, "For how long?"

"I have to leave for London eight days from now. The cottage is ours until then."

"No strings?" she asked.

"Not a one."

What she saw in his expression made her heart thunder. *How easy,* she thought, wondering why she had protested. *You don't even have to make a decision, Mariel. Or only one, and you know what that's going to be. You knew the moment you saw him again.*

His eyes followed the slow curving of her lips as she touched them with the tip of her tongue. Strange emotions coursed through her, as though this place and this man had combined to banish the transparent veils of inhibitions she hadn't even known she possessed. An eerie inevitability gripped her.

"Liar," she said softly.

He held out his hands in an odd gesture that might, had he been any other man, have represented surrender. "See what you do to me? I've never wanted a woman so much that I shook with it. Compulsion has no place in this," he told her, the angular face both primitively possessive and sharpened by hunger. "There are two bedrooms. You can choose to sleep alone if you want to, although I should tell you I'll do my best to persuade you into my bed. You can go back to the mainland—I won't try to stop you. But I want you to stay, Mariel, sweet witch."

"All right," she said huskily, not looking at him.

It was at once capitulation and approval, the gracious granting of a boon and a fierce affirmation of need, a giving and a taking—two words with all the force of a vow. She knew that Nicholas understood them, and understood her.

His arms closed tightly around her. He didn't kiss her; instead, while sensation electrified every cell in her body, he rested his cheek on her head and held her for long, silent moments. The fear and astonishment faded until she felt at peace and yet vitally renewed, acceptant of a situation made infinitely more dangerous by the swift exhilaration racing through her.

Eventually his arms loosed slightly. He said into her temple, "What do you want to do now? Eat?"

"I'd like to shower," she said unevenly.

"I'll get your case. The bedroom's on the left, third door down. There are two bathrooms—pick the one you like."

She chose the one with the huge spa bath and had to suppress a certain amount of pique when Nicholas didn't come in. Perhaps he was giving her time to become accustomed to the situation. She knew he was intelligent and experienced, but she had expected authority rather than thoughtfulness.

A thick, white wrap hung on the door; she shrugged it on smiling a little caustically as she lifted her wet hair free of the collar. It looked like a million other white bathrobes, except that it was bound with satin and the heavy toweling was of superb quality. Money might not be able to buy happiness, but it certainly provided comfort.

And as there was absolutely no doubt that Nicholas's salary wouldn't pay for this sort of luxury and seclusion, he had to be using his inheritance. It seemed appropriate.

Because it looked as though Nicholas, like his father, was intending to set up a mistress. For a fleeting moment she wondered whether he wanted more than that; whether this was a prelude to a marriage proposal.

How stupid of her heart to leap so joyously! Love and respect were the only good reasons for marriage, and she didn't love Nicholas.

And he was far too worldly to think that four days' acquaintance and a powerful sexual attraction formed any basis for marriage. No, this was to be a romantic, slightly extended version of a dirty weekend, she thought, trying to cut it down to size.

Although she was going to give this time—and herself—to him, going to sate herself with his lovemaking until she no longer craved it, she wasn't going to run the risk of ruining his career, which would happen if knowledge of an association with her became general. How happily Peter Sanderson would seize on such a piece of ''dirt'' to discredit Nicholas!

So before they burned their bridges she'd make sure Nicholas understood that this week was all they could have.

Which meant she should probably leave the cottage right now. If she was strong that was exactly what she'd do.

But she wanted this time with him so much she could feel the hunger lick through every cell in her body....

Unwinding the towel from around her head, she shook her hair back and opened a drawer in the vanity, searching for a hair dryer. Thank heavens her hair was easy to manage. She wanted to look perfect for Nicholas, wanted to give him a week he'd never forget.

Ten minutes later she walked hesitantly out into the bedroom. Nicholas must have been listening for her, because he came in from the deck, his hard face relaxing slightly when he saw her. Incredulously, she realized that he was not as confident as he seemed to be.

"I thought you'd probably prefer to unpack for yourself," he said, "but I can get the housemaid over to do it if you want me to."

"No," she said a little shyly. "Nicholas, I think we should talk before we . . . well, before we do anything irrevocable."

His eyes were watchful, but his mouth curved. "I'm glad you realize it is irrevocable," he said gently. "What do you want to say?"

Convictions were much easier to express in the privacy of the bathroom; now, with his heated green-gold eyes fixed on her face, and only too conscious of her own mounting hunger, she was tempted to give up.

But a wintry kind of integrity compelled her to say, "I don't want you to get the wrong idea. I mean, I don't want us to fool ourselves. Either of us. It wouldn't be fair when . . ."

The tangled words dried on her tongue. Motionless, he waited with the forbidding patience of a predator, his rangy figure suddenly looming very large.

Tension sparked across the taut silence. Through the subliminal thunder of her pulses came the soft call of a bird from the woods outside and the distant tinkle of the stream as it fell down a miniature waterfall. Tiny beads of moisture gathered at her temples, across her top lip and between her breasts.

"When what?" he asked unhurriedly.

She swallowed. "When it can mean nothing permanent," she said at last, each word a lash to her heart.

"Of course, you're right," he said quietly. "This is some ironic trick of the fates that's caught us both in a sensual spell. It's irrational and disturbing and bloody inconvenient, yet it's overpowering—we both seem to be helpless against it. We tried ignoring it. It didn't work for me."

She shook her head. "Nor me," she admitted.

Commanding as a raptor's gaze, his eyes held hers. "So, because neither you nor I like being held in thrall like this, we'll satisfy that hunger this week, exorcise the need, until we can see each other with some degree of clearheadedness. Is that what you wanted to say?" he asked.

That had been exactly what she intended to say. Why then, did it hurt to hear his deep voice delineating in such deliberate, dispassionate tones the boundaries of their affair?

Keeping close guard over her expression, she nodded. When she spoke her voice sounded even and unemotional. "Yes. I couldn't have put it better." She shrugged. "I want to be able to look at you and not feel this kick in my gut—not feel anything."

Had she hoped to provoke him into some kind of avowal? If so, she failed, for his only answer was a long, unwavering look as he said with cool precision, "Then we both know where we stand."

Only then did she realize how much she had wanted him to say that he had fallen madly, quixotically in love with her. His words, chosen with as much care as his diplomatic training could produce, were like small, lethal spears, killing hopes she hadn't been aware of nurturing.

I do not love him, she told that unregenerate core of romantic fantasy that lurked inside her heart. Not now, not ever!

Swiftly, before she had time to change her mind, she said, "I'm not accustomed to this sort of thing, Nicholas. I don't know exactly how to behave."

Something fierce and feral flickered in his eyes, but he said without inflection, "I don't make a habit of it, either. Now that we've established the ground rules, do you want something to eat?"

"No, thank you," she said. "I had something on the plane."

And then at last he moved, releasing his powerful body from the leashed, watchful stasis she found so intimidating. Mariel's breath lodged in her throat. Her eyes, ensnared by the glinting golden lights in his, dilated.

When he spoke his voice was slightly raw, as though she'd breached his formidable self-possession at last. "Then perhaps you need a rest?"

Striving to retain some objectivity, she cataloged the sensations that assailed her—the shaft of lightning down her spine, the simultaneous meltdown in her bones, the heated heaviness that uncurled in the pit of her stomach and moved in languorous waves through her, robbing her of will and energy.

And yet a different energy, more primitive and basic than any other, began to throb through her, white-hot and consuming. Calling up her last atom of sanity, she touched her tongue to suddenly dry lips and said in a stifled voice, "Nicholas, I'm not on the pill."

"I'll take care of that," he said, his gaze settling on her mouth as though it held the assurance of bliss. A lean forefinger found the throbbing little traitor in her throat. "I'll take care of everything," he promised, the words slow and deliberate. "Everything you want, Mariel, everything you need. Tell me and I'll do it, I'll give it to you..."

"I want you." Unable to meet the brilliance of his glance, her weighted eyelids drifted down. She felt her mouth widen in a temptress's smile, enduring as womanhood, more easily understood than speech. "All of you. Everything. That's all I want."

How long did they stand there, joined only by his hand across her throat? She thought she could feel his life force connect with hers from the warmth of his palm, the sensitive tips of his fingers.

And then he made a guttural sound deep in his chest and pulled her into him, holding her fast against a body taut with need.

When she tilted her face in mute, unconscious invitation, he kissed her with the starving intensity of a man too long denied sustenance, an intensity she not only reciprocated but met and matched, opening her mouth eagerly for his passionate invasion, feeling the last stronghold inside her shatter and break beneath the overpowering impact of his sexuality and her own.

Lifting his head, he looked at her with blazing eyes, his face hard and demanding. "You are everything *I* need," he said quietly.

And to her amazement he picked her up and carried her across to the bed, lowering her onto the coverlet. She wriggled to free herself of the robe, but he said, "No, let me," and without haste pulled it from her, his eyes glittering with self-imposed restraint.

"Like unwrapping a present," he said.

When she was naked, her body exposed to the heated intensity of his gaze, a tide of peach lapped up through her skin, because he looked at her as though she was the personification of all he'd ever longed for.

"I knew you would be like this," he said harshly. "Siren and sorceress...'the depth and dream of my desire'... Mariel, beautiful, ivory, gleaming Mariel, I think I've been waiting for you all my life."

He bent and kissed her throat, and then the soft contour of her breast. His mouth was so hot she thought his lips would leave marks like the golden kisses of a god, but all that stained her skin was the slow wave of color.

For the first time ever she wanted to revel in the effect her body had on a man; with David she had been self-conscious, but now embarrassment was the furthest thing from her mind. In Nicholas's eyes and hands and mouth there was nothing but hunger, an admiration that came close to awe and a passion so intense she felt scorched by it.

In a voice she barely recognized as her own she said, "This isn't fair. You still have your clothes on."

"Take them off, then."

For a moment she froze, but although his face revealed an imperious authority, she discerned laughter in his eyes. Almost immediately, her breath stopping in her throat, she saw the laughter swallowed by need.

Trying to stop her hands from shaking, she reached up and slid the buttons of his shirt open, gazing greedily and with something of his awe at the expanse of copper skin she'd uncovered, fine-grained and sleek, lightly covered with hair in an age-old pattern. She pushed the fine cloth of the shirt back from his shoulders and lifted herself to kiss what she'd revealed.

It was then that she understood the full extent of her power over him. There was no disguising his sharp intake of breath when her mouth lingered on his skin, or the sudden increase of tension caused by her caress.

Astonished, she looked up. His eyes were agonized, his mouth disciplined into a hard, straight line, but when her wondering eyes met his he smiled and said on a harsh note, "It works both ways, Mariel. My mouth on your skin, yours on mine—and the foundations of the earth are ripped apart."

She whispered, "I didn't know," and hesitated.

"Don't stop now," he said with gritted teeth. "I might just die with the torment, but don't stop."

When at last the shirt had joined her bathrobe on the floor, she looked at him with slumberous eyes and murmured, "You are so beautiful."

He smiled. "I should be saying that."

"No." She trailed a finger down to where his chest hair narrowed into a point, followed the thin arrow toward his trousers. "I know I'm not beautiful, but oh, Nicholas, you are."

"How can you look at yourself in the mirror and say you're not beautiful? 'All made of fantasy, all made of passion,'" he quoted.

Infected by his taut expectancy, she shivered, her courage evaporating like rain in the sun. His hand covered hers as she went to withdraw it.

"Don't pull away," he said unsteadily.

It took all her courage, but eventually she managed to undo the zip and push his trousers down over his hips. Resting her cheek against his chest, she thrilled to the heavy pounding of his heart, and knew there could be no going back.

And then he whispered her name, and lifted her head and held her face between two strong-fingered hands and looked at her, the golden rays in his eyes submerged in a rush of purest green. His mouth was twisted.

"I knew the moment I set eyes on you that you were trouble. Blue-eyed, soft-mouthed, long-legged trouble," he said, and laughed and kissed her, almost tenderly at first, and then with such power that she was swept away in a flood of eroticism.

In a moment she was on her back, her hands sliding across the heated skin of his shoulders, her body arched so that her hips pressed against his in an assertion as explicit as it was demanding.

"Yes," he said deeply.

He tore his clothes off, revealing narrow hips and long, well-muscled legs, and a jutting member that proclaimed his readiness.

When Mariel gasped he smiled dangerously.

"We'll fit," he said, and bent over her, tasting the small dimple of her navel, his mouth lingering on her skin. "You'll see—we'll fit perfectly."

He was right, but he made her wait before she experienced that perfect joining. In spite of the desperate compulsion of their mutual ardor, he took his time, lying with her in the silver-gilt fingers of the sunlight on the big four-poster bed and exploring, touching, telling her what he wanted, insisting she do the same.

At first she kept her eyes closed, her lips sealed except for kisses. David had been a silent lover; Nicholas's demands that she tell him her most secret fantasies seemed an intrusion, but he coaxed responses from her, gentling her with his hands and his mouth and his tone until she began to answer.

Oh, God, he was skillful, a conqueror in a war where both sides won, an expert in the art of reducing a woman to shaking, shivering helplessness, so completely at his mercy, so greedy for what only he could give her that Mariel would have followed him anywhere, with her heart in her hand.

He made himself master of her body, but he insisted that she in turn make herself utterly familiar with his. When at last she was sobbing for him, wanting only that one thing he had promised her, the complete satisfaction of the hunger that ripped her composure into shreds, there was not an ounce of restraint left in her.

Wild-eyed, she gloried in the beads of sweat across his brow, the subtle prominence of the bones of his face, and was fiercely glad that his studied consideration had been vanquished by an overwhelming, consuming craving. At least she was not the only one so affected; Nicholas, too, was desperate for this, starving for it.

And then he moved, and she arched again, taking him in, enclosing him, her whole being glorying in the sensations as he pushed home.

Shuddering, she tightened her muscles instinctively, drawing him farther up, clamping so that he couldn't withdraw.

"No," he said in a strained voice, "don't do that, Mariel, don't..."

But she couldn't stop herself, and instantly he responded, driving into her in a rhythm that sent the waves of sensation surging out from her center, increasing in strength, building with each movement, each deep thrust, until eventually she fell into an implosion of delight, of rapture, of joy so piercing she couldn't control her choked cry.

Nicholas laughed and flung his head back. Never before had Mariel seen a man in the throes of ecstasy; her eyes darkened even further as the fierce angularity of his features dissolved into ferocious pleasure.

She couldn't catch the words he groaned as the rigidity of his body eased into lassitude, into satiation. Hips and thighs locked together, heart beating against heart, she held him against her, wonder and astonishment and a lazy, languid repletion thickening her blood into honey, until he lifted his head and turned onto his side, taking her with him so that she lay half over him, her head on his shoulder.

What can I say? she thought in a sudden foolish panic. *Thank you? How stupid, but I can't just lie here. I used to tell David that I loved him, but that isn't appropriate for Nicholas. What do you say to a man who has shown you the sun?*

"There's a Spanish proverb: Take what you want, says God, and pay for it," Nicholas said quietly. "If it's true, I have hell waiting for me sometime in the future."

She shivered. "Life doesn't even out like that," she said. "Life is chaotic, without order. Dreadful things happen to wonderful people, and terrible people die at a ripe old age."

"So you don't believe in karma, or that what you sow you'll reap."

"Not really." She thought about it for a moment. "I suppose I believe that you have to do the best you can," she said slowly, watching the sunlight dance through the open door, "and leave the rest to the power that runs this universe." A yawn stretched her mouth. Covering it, she mumbled, "I'm sorry."

"Why? Don't apologize for things you can't help. Why don't you go to sleep? Or would you like a shower, or something to drink?"

"A drink would be nice."

When he'd gone she lay thinking, trying to impose some order on her own personal chaos. Nothing had ever been like that before.

Nothing.

And in her inner heart she knew it was all wrong. She had loved David with all her heart, and he had loved her—oh, not enough to put her ahead of his career, but that didn't alter his emotions. He had been a tender and considerate lover, and she had enjoyed making love with him.

Nicholas didn't even pretend to love her; he'd spoken of satisfying a need, a wild, uncontrollable lust that he could appease only by indulging it.

She had hoped for a future with David, but right from the start she'd known that there was no future for her with Nicholas. She knew and accepted that the attraction between them was purely physical, a matter of hormones and chemistry, the primal desire of a healthy woman of breeding age for a virile man of high standing. Darwin had called it natural selection, the mindless urge to reproduce, to produce babies who were fit and strong and would keep the race going.

When she made love with David her whole heart had been involved, yet in Nicholas's arms she had encountered something that made the pleasure she'd found with David a pallid, lifeless thing, a mild response to a need she couldn't even recall now.

What she had shared with Nicholas had been a true communion, a loss of boundaries so that he had become part of her and she of him.

And that, her cynical mind told her, was dangerously sentimental thinking. Such striving to give some mystical importance to what had simply been a very enjoyable experience was nothing but foolishness.

The romantic vision of one perfect partner was a delusion; she had seen many marriages begin with love and hope only to descend into disillusionment and divorce. Conversely, she knew people whose first happy marriage had been destroyed by death, and who had then gone on to forge another, equally satisfying relationship. The belief in and search for the ideal mate was simply a way of avoiding responsibility for working hard at a marriage.

After all, she had truly thought that in David she had found the one man who would make her happy. She had loved him with passion and respect and liking, and she had thought her life was over when he left her.

But she had recovered.

Now she was slowly coming to realize that there were other forms of bondage every bit as powerful as love, and perhaps even more difficult to break away from.

Nicholas interrupted her tumbling confusion. "Lime juice," he said as he came through the door holding a glass. "It's fresh."

"Thank you," she said, unable to hold back another yawn.

He laughed and sat on the edge of the bed while she drank it, then lay down with her and held her until they both slid into sleep, entwined bodies bonelessly sleek and contented as cats in the sun.

When she awoke again it was with the steady thud of his heart beneath her cheek. Slowly she lifted her head and watched him, marveling at the way his dark lashes shadowed his skin.

After this week she would have to ruthlessly cut herself free from Nicholas. Instinct warned her that if she continued seeing him, it wouldn't be long before she lost her heart completely.

And that would lead to far more pain than she'd experienced when David dumped her. Beside the man who was now her lover, David appeared weak and ineffectual, his gentleness revealed to be a sort of moral cowardice. She had survived his betrayal; if she fell in love with Nicholas she might well be permanently damaged.

His breathing changed. Smiling, she kissed his shoulder.

"Mmm," he said intelligently, and yawned.

A slight noise made her lift her head. "What's that?"

"The housekeeper preparing an evening meal."

Of course. She said, "I could do that."

"It won't be much of a holiday for you if you have to cook."

She cuddled closer, her body still lethargic and replete. "I quite like cooking and, anyway, you can help."

Hard mouth softening in a smile, he ran a hand down her spine, causing a swift shiver of delight. "I make superb scrambled eggs," he said, "but that's the sum total of my cooking prowess."

She nipped his skin with sharp white teeth. "It's time you learned more, then. I'd rather we didn't have to bother with staff."

"All right. We'll wait until she's done whatever she needs to now and then I'll tell her not to come back."

"How much food is there in the pantry?"

"How do I know?" he said. "Don't worry, we can get more. I won't let you starve."

She traced the hard swell of his muscle with her tongue. "It sounds like paradise," she said throatily.

"Almost as close as humanity can come to it," he said, and bent his head and kissed her breast.

CHAPTER SEVEN

"WHY AREN'T YOU MARRIED?" she asked three days later, smiling at him from a rug beneath the dappled shade of a tree. "I thought diplomats were encouraged to marry."

"They are." Bare-chested and bare-legged, wearing a pair of shorts that had seen better days, he was sitting in a deck chair, eyes shielded from the sun by dark glasses. "The pressure's not overt, however, and I don't take any notice of it."

"Such arrogance." She laughed.

It was the same arrogance—unintentional, she was learning, but very much there—that had led him to veto sitting out on the beach with the words "New Zealanders don't travel for beaches. We have the best beaches in the world."

If she was planning a future with him, she thought now, ignoring the odd little ache in her heart, she'd have to do something about that attitude. As it was, it wasn't going to matter to her.

Besides, although the beach was deserted, she wouldn't be comfortable lying as she was now, body bared entirely to the warm, salty air. Three days and nights of Nicholas's lovemaking had freed her of all inhibitions with him, but she couldn't imagine sunbathing nude on a public beach.

Yawning, she turned onto her side. "I read in a magazine article that men who don't marry by the time they're thirty often don't marry at all."

His brows lifting, he surveyed her sun-glazed body. "If you read a book occasionally, instead of magazines, you'd know that often the articles are wrong," he said austerely.

She grinned. "I do read books. And don't avoid the issue. Why aren't you married?"

"Because I've never met anyone I wanted to live with for the rest of my life," he said calmly.

And that, of course, included her. The past few days had been an idyll. Cut off from everything but themselves, they had reveled unashamedly in sensuality, taking carnal enjoyment in each other's bodies, eating when they were hungry, spending much of their time either in bed or outside beside the pool, always with the unspoken understanding that they were there for only one thing—the heated desire that so far remained unsated.

"Nobody? Your standards must be incredibly high."

He shrugged. "Perhaps. I was born of an adulterous liaison, so I learned from an early age that marriage isn't necessary."

She looked uncertainly at him. Until that moment he'd said nothing about his childhood. "Was it hard on you?" she asked.

"No. For years I just took everything for granted, and by the time I realized what the situation was, I was old enough to understand. My father was tied to a wife who couldn't give him children and who wasn't in love with him."

Mariel waited for Nicholas to continue, but when it became evident that he wasn't going to, she asked, "It seems strange that they didn't divorce."

"They belonged to a religion in which divorce was banned, and there were financial aspects, as well. I think he'd have liked to have lived with my mother, but she found her life eminently satisfying as it was. She was an artist, a very well-known one, and a full-time husband would probably have been a nuisance."

"What about a full-time child?" Mariel asked dryly.

"The child had a full-time nanny," he said, sounding both amused and surprised at her perception. "And was much happier than you were—I wasn't sensitive, and my nanny loved me. My mother did, too, in her own way, and my father never made any bones about it."

Although he always spoke of his parents with affection, there seemed to be an equivocal inflection to his words that said in some way he despised them both. Mariel wanted to know why, wanted to know all about him, but there were barriers she didn't feel brave enough to tackle.

Besides, it was none of her business, she told herself, watching him from beneath her lashes.

He stretched luxuriously, muscles and bones popping, copper skin flexing over the lean strength that knew how to take her to ecstasy.

Something primitive and forbidden uncurled in Mariel's gut. By now, she thought, looking back over the past days, she should be at least accustomed to him, the keen edge of her hunger blunted a little.

Instead, she had only to look at him to feel that bone-deep desire, as though her need was fed by the joyous, unhampered power of their lovemaking. She couldn't get enough of him, and it seemed her feelings were entirely reciprocated.

"Tell me about your childhood," he said. "How did your parents die?"

She'd been expecting it, so she was as ready as she was ever likely to be. Trying to ignore the telltale trickle of ice down her spine, she said lightly, "There's not a lot to tell. They were killed in an accident, and I went back to New Zealand to live with my aunt."

"In the small town in the King Country." Her startled look brought a smile to his beautifully chiseled mouth, an imperceptible softening of the green-gold gaze. "You told me that right at the start when I was busy trying to immunize myself against you."

"Why did you want to do that?" It was sheer self-indulgence to ask, and she knew the moment she'd said the words that she'd made a mistake.

His smile was derisive, his tone caustic. "Oh, for some reason I've always been drawn to long-legged, sleek-skinned redheads with eyes that tilt very slightly at the corners, and I find it vaguely distasteful that my hormones should have such control over me."

Mariel did, too. It reduced their lovemaking to a mechanical, sex-driven coupling that was ugly and sordid. With a snap of her voice she said, "So you did your best to warn me off."

"Exactly," he said.

Well, she already knew how important being in control was to him. Why should she feel so let down? After all, right from the start she had told herself that *her* feelings for *him* were solely physical.

But she was changing, and it hurt that he so obviously wasn't. Oh, the sexual need was still terrifyingly powerful, but other, reluctant feelings had burgeoned—respect, and an admiration that was not sexual at all. Without realizing it, she had hoped the same thing was happening to him.

Rolling onto her back, she presented her profile to him for a second before covering her face with her hat.

"But of course I couldn't banish you from my mind," he said calmly. "Every time I turned around you were there. Worse than that, I found myself making opportunities to be with you. And then I saw you dealing so efficiently with the trade ministers and hotel staff and so very gently with that little girl, saw how you gritted your teeth and kept your head and refused to be intimidated when her father was waving his gun around, and I began to wonder whether the previous women had been merely preludes to you."

"I'll bet you say that to all the long-legged redheads," she said in a muffled voice.

"I could tell you that this time it's different, but you wouldn't believe me, would you?"

"Probably not." It took a real effort, but she thought she managed the right lazily dismissive tone, as though the subject bored her.

"You were very busy doing exactly the same with me. You did your best to ignore me completely."

"I," she said, forgetting to be cool about it, "do not make a habit of falling for every tall, athletic, green-eyed man who comes along."

He laughed softly. "Perhaps not, but I could see the barricades crash into place every time you looked at me."

"Did it pique your interest?" The question positively crackled.

"In other words, did I decide to seduce you to prove my power. What do you think, Mariel?"

Although he sounded no more than mildly interested, his voice self-possessed and deep and speculative, she didn't make the mistake of thinking he wasn't angry.

Ashamed because she'd been angling for another answer, one he wasn't going to give, she said, "I know you didn't."

Apparently apropos of nothing, Nicholas said quietly, "My mother told me once that women invariably choose the most powerful men they can attract, because until very recently male power has been one of the attributes that would help their children survive. She read a book on the Middle Ages that gave a breakdown on infant deaths in the various classes—aristocracy, merchants and peasants—and there was no doubt that the aristocracy, and the upper echelons especially, had a disproportionate number of children survive the rigors of infancy."

Intrigued, yet a little indignant, Mariel suggested, "Surely it was because they were better fed and better housed."

"That," he countered, "is what a secure, high-paying job promises, doesn't it?"

She said, "Are you insinuating that I'm materialistic?"

"No, and I'm not insinuating that you want to marry me—after all, we know that's not true, don't we?—but according to my mother's theory most women unconsciously find a good provider sexy and desirable as a mate."

She opened her lips, then closed them again, glad that he couldn't see beneath the straw hat.

However, he said evenly, "Yes, I know what you're thinking. My mother would say that, wouldn't she, when you consider her life and her relationship with my father. I'm not saying I believe her theory, either, although it does make some sense. I do think that your propensity for diplomats and mine for women of a certain type of coloring and form is merely a propensity. I don't imagine that you see every diplomat you meet as a possible husband, and although I might feel a moment of attraction when I meet a woman, I promise you I don't leap into bed with everyone who fits the pattern."

She said waspishly, "Only the ones you like?"

His amusement was tinged with irony. "No. In spite of the way I've behaved these last few days, I can usually control myself. It's only that first moment, the physical impact that affects me. Normally I look past the hair and the eyes and the legs and see the woman behind, and that involuntary flicker of desire dies."

She didn't want to ask, but the words wouldn't be leashed. "Did that happen with me?"

"Fishing, Mariel?" His voice was enigmatic; she'd have given anything to see his face, but dared not remove the hat. Beneath it, heat crawled across her skin, flooded from her breasts to her throat in a prickly, damning surge.

He said judicially, "For the first time ever I couldn't control my reactions. In fact, for a while I thought I was losing my grip, going slightly mad. I wanted you so much I could taste it. You invaded my dreams, and thinking of you took up far too much of my waking time. That had never happened to me before."

"You were as nasty as you could be." Yes, her voice was fine—steady, slightly humorous, with no more than a hint of censure.

"I was not nasty," he said firmly. "I was quietly racing into desperation. I tried to establish a respectable distance between us, only to discover to my chagrin that I couldn't. I kept making excuses to see you, wondering what you were doing, looking around jealously to see who you were with."

"So you decided you'd find a way to rid yourself of this inconvenient itch, and you organized this idyll. What would you have done if I'd said thanks, but no thanks?"

"It sounds conceited, but I was reasonably sure you wouldn't."

"Conceit has nothing to do with it," she said. "You must have been certain of my answer. That last night here, a month ago, I offered myself to you on a plate. I thought I'd disgusted you. I certainly disgusted myself."

He leaned over and pulled her up onto his lap, exerting his great strength with an ease that always awed her. Her hat and his glasses tumbled unnoticed to the ground as his hands slid around her throat, pushing her chin up with his thumbs so he could look into her shamed eyes.

"That night was...like something out of the *Arabian Nights,* like an exotic fantasy come true. I've never liked women who come on to men, even though I'll admit there's no reason they shouldn't. I've always thought I valued subtlety. But that night you blew my mind. You were everything I'd ever wanted in a woman, and I didn't know how to cope with it. I only knew that I couldn't behave as though you were a simple one-night stand. To do that would be to devalue what we felt. And I thought, I don't need this. I can't handle it. I don't want to handle it." His mouth tightened. "Besides, I was sure it would soon fade."

That hurt, too.

"Great minds think alike," she countered.

"But we were wrong, weren't we. I think I knew, even when I was organizing this week, that a simple sating of honest lust wasn't going to work," he said softly. "I didn't want to admit it, of course." He paused, the glittering gold in his eyes suddenly blazing forth hypnotically. In words that seemed torn from him he said quickly, "Mariel, marry me."

Temptation dug its fingers into her heart, into her brain, whispering siren words that eroded her willpower like a flood over an earthen dam. "No," she said rigidly. "Oh, no, don't. *Please.*"

"Why not? We both know by now that, wonderful though the sex is, this is much more than that. Can you just turn your back on it and walk away?"

Unable to bear looking at him, she closed her eyes, shaking her head. "You don't want to marry me. We agreed, remember, this was to get it out of our systems...."

"We were idiots. Look at me, Mariel."

When she refused, squeezing her eyes shut so that tiny red dots sparked behind her lids and began to whirl, he said on a note of gritty amusement, "You can't behave like a child told to do something she doesn't want to. Refusing to open your eyes isn't going to change anything."

There was an element of denial in her reaction, but mostly she wanted to be free of the wicked enchantment of his glance, the hard promise of his mouth. Reluctantly, her whole being shouting danger, she lifted her lashes and focused on him.

He smiled, although his eyes were now coolly, purely green. His hand lifted, came to rest on the lush curve of her breast. "See how dark my skin is against yours," he said with quiet, heart-stopping insistence. "Dark and pale together. I could spend the rest of my life looking at that contrast, and I swear every time I do I'll want you. Are you sated, Mariel?"

She couldn't breathe, couldn't move, locked in a stillness broken only by the throbbing of her nerve ends at the slow movement of his fingers. She whispered, "No, I'm not sated."

"Then marry me, and we'll devote the rest of our lives to seeing if it can be done."

Her breath came sharply. She covered his hand with hers, pressing it against her heart, and said unevenly, "Sex isn't love, Nicholas. And love is the only reason for marriage."

"Whatever we have is something worth fighting for. We talk together, we argue without fighting, we enjoy each other's company.... Oh, I'll admit I wondered whether we'd tire of each other when we'd made love, when all the excitement of the preliminary fencing was over, but I find your mind infinitely fascinating. And is it too conceited of me to believe that you enjoy my company as much as I enjoy yours?"

She scrambled off his lap; for a moment his hands tightened cruelly on her waist, indenting the fine skin, and she was pinned, held captive, until he swore under his breath and let her go. Her heart was slowly shattering in her chest, fragmenting into millions of painful shards amidst the ruins of her life.

"You know I do," she muttered, "but I can't marry you."

"Can't?" His voice was harsh. "Or won't?"

She should say that she wouldn't. Then he would hate her and perhaps get over her more quickly. But even as she toyed with the idea she knew she couldn't do it. He wouldn't believe her, anyway; that astute brain had picked up on the small clues that gave her away.

Besides, she owed him the truth.

And when she told him he would no longer want to marry her. In fact, he would probably despise her.

"I should have left as soon as I realized that you'd brought me here," she said raggedly. "Because I knew then—I've always known—that there's no future for us.

Nicholas, my parents were Joy and Gordon Frensham. You must have heard of them. Twenty years ago they were posted to the New Zealand Embassy in Hong Kong. Three years later they were accused of spying for the Soviets. They committed suicide before any case could be brought against them, but apparently there was no doubt about their guilt. What would it do to your career to marry their daughter?''

She heard him stand up, but kept her face turned resolutely away.

"Why tell me now?" he asked in a voice so icily measured it chilled her through.

"I don't go around telling people," she said wearily. "I'm not proud of what they did. They ruined not only their own lives but my aunt's, as well. She had a career in the diplomatic service, was well on the way to becoming New Zealand's first woman ambassador, and she had to resign. Mud sticks, Nicholas. If I married you it would ruin your career, too, because there are still people in positions of power who remember them. Just as there are people who would use me against you. Peter Sanderson, for instance."

"I can deal with the Sandersons of this world," he said arrogantly.

She shook her head. "It would ruin you, Nicholas."

"Mariel, it would not—"

Tears gathered on her lashes, clogged her throat. "I know it would. When I told David, he consulted his parents and his old headmaster and his uncle—Sir Richard Greville, the British ambassador in Germany, who should know if anyone does—and they all said marrying me would be fatal for his prospects."

"Oh, for God's sake, they're a pack of old—"

"I won't marry you," she said firmly. "And when you've thought about it, you'll agree it would be impossible."

"Mariel, I knew who you were before you left the island a month ago."

She felt her mouth drop. "What?" she whispered, her head jerking up.

He was watching her with narrowed eyes, his face hard and alert and determined. "One of the older members of the group recognized you," he said.

"The security guard," she said numbly. "At the gym."

"Yes, Ogilvie. You look like your father, apparently—same coloring, same bone structure. And you move your head in certain ways and use the same expression. Ogilvie was sure he knew who you were, but you weren't calling yourself Frensham. Security men being security men, suspicious to the core, he checked your dossier with Forsythe, the hotel head of security, purely as a precaution. It stood up to scrutiny, but he wasn't satisfied, so he got on the line to New Zealand. After that it didn't take much time to find out what had happened to you and who you were. The day the minister ordered me to take you out to dinner I'd just been told that you were almost certainly the daughter of the Frenshams."

"Was that why Ogilvie interrupted us by the staircase?" Another memory struck her. "While you were talking to him Peter Sanderson came up and tried to get me to go to the nightclub. Did he know?"

"Of course he didn't," Nicholas said.

For some reason that comforted her.

"And yes, that was why Ogilvie called me away. He and Forsythe had gone through your dossier with a fine-tooth comb before Ogilvie got on the line to Wellington. Once Wellington got back to me and confirmed that you were definitely their daughter, he sent Susan Waterhouse down to the bar to confirm it."

"So I was automatically tarred with the same brush," she said bitterly.

Exasperation sharpened his words. "Admit it, Mariel—it did look suspicious. You weren't using their name, you

certainly weren't telling anyone who you were, and you were
in a position to gather information."

"So spying has to run in the genes. Did the minister decide that you should take me out to dinner and use your
powerful masculine magnetism to pump me?" Better a sneer
than a wail of agony!

The hesitation was so brief she almost missed it, but she
had come to know him over these past few days. "Yes, he
did."

And she thought Mr. McCabe had been kind! Just another small disillusion amongst so many, and yet it hurt almost as much as Nicholas's part in the situation. Perhaps
she was concentrating on the lesser pain to spare herself the
anguish of the greater. "Ply me with wine, perhaps kiss me
several times so that I wasn't thinking clearly, and then ask
the question and watch my face?"

He shrugged. "Possibly that's what he had in mind. Now
you can see why I was so angry, why I asked those bloody
intrusive questions. I knew I was strongly attracted to you,
I was fighting it, and here I was being ordered to use that
attraction to get information from you. I felt like a heel."

"But you did it," she said stonily.

"I did it." The harsh contours of his face defeated her
accusing glance. "Partly because I wanted to take you out,
wanted to kiss you, but mostly because, if it turned out you
were spying for whatever reason, I was sure the knowledge
would kill whatever it was I felt for you. Only I blew it
properly, stumbling over the crudest of queries with all the
finesse of an ant in a sugar bowl because I was repelled by
what I had to do, and because all I really wanted to know
was how much that bloody St. Clair meant to you."

Silently she considered his words, trying hard to fan the
tiny flicker of hope in her heart. But she knew that she
couldn't; he wanted her, and with his natural arrogance he
thought he could bend the world to his bidding. Unfortunately life didn't work that way.

She said dully, "It doesn't really matter. It's impossible." The water in the pool shimmered in her eyes. Urgently, giving him no time to speak, she said, "David was—is—as ambitious as you are and he did love me, Nicholas. He didn't give in easily. But in the end, the real world, the one we live in, not this idyll you've created for us here, broke his dreams."

Nicholas came up and put his hands on her shoulders, twisting her around so that he could see into her face. His own was serious, the blazing eyes hooded, his mouth firm. "He was a coward," he said quietly. "Darling, trust me."

Grief splintered through her, robbing the world of all warmth, all color, all joy, but from somewhere she summoned the grim endurance to continue.

"It's not a matter of trust." She turned her head and kissed the strong wrist, leaning her cheek against it because that way she could keep her face averted.

"Then what..." Irritation and anger sounded in his voice.

"Don't make it any harder for me, please," she interrupted. "I am the daughter of two traitors. I believe the information they sold to the Soviets led directly to the deaths of at least half-a-dozen agents, American, as well as British. Governments have long memories, and diplomats' wives are vetted almost as carefully as their husbands. If we marry, your career path is going to be much rockier than it need be. I'm right, aren't I?"

He hesitated, considering her words. Then he said shortly, "It could, I suppose."

Oh, he was different from David. No swift protestations, no facile promises.

Now, she told her heart. *One last blow and then you can die.* "Do you think I could bear knowing I had done that to you?"

"You're overreacting."

Tears burned at the back of her eyes. "It's no use," she whispered. "I know how much you love your career. Mr.

McCabe told me you have a great future in the corps. I can't jeopardize that.''

"I see." Merciless eyes pierced the sorry rags of her self-possession and stabbed right into her soul.

She held them for only a moment, because she couldn't allow him to see how much this was hurting her. He was a good man, and later, when he realized how impossible the situation was, it would worry him to know how much pain she was feeling.

"I'll leave straight away," he said without expression, "but there is, of course, no reason for you to go. The cottage is at your disposal until the end of the week."

Unevenly, stupidly, she said, "Nicholas, no. It doesn't have to be like this."

His brows shot up. "What are you offering?" he asked courteously.

She bit her lip. "I . . . we could . . ."

He didn't help, simply stood there looking at her with a flat, lethal gaze.

Mariel swallowed. "We don't have to call it all off," she said, endeavoring to sound normal, to hide the fact that she was dying inside. Against everything sensible, against her compulsion to protect him, she said, "We could still see each other," even as she was horrified at the reckless need that had summoned the words from the depths of her heart.

"Conduct a long-distance love affair?" he said with cutting politeness. "See each other every three months or so when our paths coincide? Is that what you want, Mariel? A nice, convenient lover who doesn't clutter up your life? I don't have the same outlook as my mother. I wouldn't find much joy in that."

She dragged a deep, painful breath into her lungs, striving for composure. "You're right," she said after a moment. "It was a stupid thing to say."

"Very," he said.

Pride raised her head, kept her voice cool and even slightly mocking. "So it's all or nothing?"

"I prefer a quick, clean death to a lingering decline," he said, and turned and walked away from her, sun gleaming red on his hair, highlighting the angular features, the disciplined grace.

It was then, as Nicholas strode out of her life, that she admitted she'd been fooling herself. She'd fallen into the oldest trap in the world, one baited with her heart, and now she was a prisoner behind the bars of her needs and her emotions. She didn't just want him, she loved him, and because her parents had been greedy and treacherous twenty years before she was never going to have him.

She had loved David, and she grieved when he left her, but it had been nothing like this. This pain wrenched her whole body, tore at her heart, numbed her mind. Shivering, she wrapped a huge beach towel around her and walked into the woods, farther and farther into the shadows until she was stopped by a large live oak. She put her forearms against the trunk and stood with her face pressed into them, too spent to cry, too wounded to do anything but bear the agony.

HE LEFT NOTHING behind, not even a note.

But two weeks later Carole said, "Oh, by the way, a letter arrived with the check for your week at Bride's Bay."

Mariel frowned. Resentment struggled with relief; at least she wouldn't have to explain any lack of payment but she hated feeling beholden to him. "A letter?" she asked, wondering just what Nicholas had done now.

Carole sent her a bright-eyed glance. "Yes. With 'Personal' stamped on the envelope."

He had sent her double her usual fee; the note said negligently, "Dear Mariel, Please accept this. I wish you well in your future life."

He was hers, N.

She gave the money to a charity and tore the note up, then spent half of one sleepless night reassembling it with glue on a sheet of tissue paper.

Mariel thought she knew about pain and grief, about the bitterness of losing everything she'd ever wanted, but in the following weeks she discovered that David's betrayal had only scratched the surface. Even the memory of the anguish following her parents' deaths paled. As she went mechanically about her job she found that her capacity for heartache was limitless, rooted in the depths of her love.

Unable to eat or sleep, she lost seven pounds and gained two new lines in her face, until at last a friend's shocked exclamations persuaded her to force food down her reluctant throat, and for the first time in her life to enlist the help of sleeping pills. It took her weeks to reestablish some sort of sleep pattern so that she could give them up. Unfortunately, without them she dreamed—wild fantasies of Nicholas that slid swiftly into erotic illusions from which she awoke aching and heated, her body racked with hunger, her mind in chaos.

Two MONTHS after she'd left the cottage on Jermain Island, Mariel was walking out of the Metropolitan Museum of Art in Manhattan when she saw him. Dry-mouthed, her mind suddenly feverish with hope, she stopped at the top of the steps, watching as he strode down in front of her.

Pain squeezed her hammering heart. She would know Nicholas anywhere, the set of his broad shoulders, the smooth, masculine grace of his movements. As she watched, the woman beside him stumbled slightly and, laughing, clutched at him. His arm whipped out, caught her around the waist and supported her until they reached the street.

She was a long-legged, stylishly dressed redhead, a woman whose mouth didn't strike Mariel as being particularly soft. Susan Waterhouse.

Nausea and a bitter surge of jealousy raked through her. Bitter as a woman wronged, she stood like Galatea encased in marble and watched them walk down past the lions and out onto the street. They turned toward Central Park.

"You all right?" a voice asked with the automatic wariness of a native New Yorker.

"Yes." Turning her head, Mariel's eyes met the concerned, cautious glance of a young woman some years younger. "Just indigestion," she lied. "I've taken something for it—I'll be fine in a few minutes."

"Can I get you a cab?"

"No, I'll just wait here for a few minutes. Thank you."

"You're welcome," the woman said automatically, and walked on down the steps. At the bottom she turned and looked back.

Warmed by her concern, Mariel waved. The woman waved back and went on her way, leaving Mariel to turn her head so that she could watch Nicholas and Susan walk into the park. Only half an hour ago she'd stood in the museum by the windows that looked out on the park and seen summer lovers strolling and flirting, family groups chatting and calling out admonitions to laughing children, all grateful for the lush oasis in the midst of the city.

Oh, God, she thought, unable to move until Nicholas and Susan had disappeared beneath the green of the trees.

Such pain could not be endured, and yet somehow she managed to find strength enough to make her way to the curb and hail a cab.

Back in her apartment she sat for a long time, hugging herself with her arms, trying to erase the image of Nicholas and Susan as they walked down the steps together. There had been something so...easy, she thought despairingly, about the way they touched each other, so familiar and right.

She fought the corrosion of jealousy. If she really loved Nicholas, she would want him to be happy, even if his happiness meant that he married another woman. "I do," she said out loud, her voice strained and unnaturally high. "Of course I want him to be happy."

But she didn't want him to marry anyone else but her!

Nicholas and Susan must be in New York for the conference on international trade sponsored by the United Nations. Everyone who had any sort of interest in the subject at all was there, busy trying to push their own agenda.

Mariel had refused to read about it in the newspapers, hadn't allowed herself to even think about the possibility of Nicholas's being there, but perhaps she should have.

No, not all the mental preparation in the world would have made it easier to see them together. And rather than be haunted by how relaxed they were with each other, why not blame the whim of malevolent fate that had made her walk out of the museum after them? Of all the places in New York, she thought wearily, why did she have to see him there? From now on the place would be haunted by his tall figure, the arrogant poise of his dark head, the smooth, effortless walk.

CAROLE CALLED the next morning, waking Mariel from the too-deep sleep that comes from not dropping off until almost dawn.

"Yes, I know it's the weekend," she said when Mariel croaked a complaint into the receiver, "but this is an emergency. An interpreter has got some sort of vicious bug, and we've been asked for someone who speaks Mandarin and French."

"What about Gee-Ling?"

"She's already booked up solid."

Mariel said resignedly, "Oh, all right." It would stop her from worrying about what Nicholas and Susan were doing.

The meeting, held in a hotel not far from the United Nations building, began at lunchtime, and the negotiations didn't wind down until eight that night. It certainly kept her mind off herself; by the time it finished she was utterly exhausted.

At least, she thought, waiting as the doorman called a cab, she would sleep tonight. No more highly colored nightmares of Nicholas and Susan entwined together in the throes of passion, no memories of Nicholas's face as he reached his climax, the agonized starkness of his features, mouth drawn tight, the way his head went back at the moment of greatest pleasure....

And no more memories of his beloved weight, the scent of his skin that was more precious than attar of roses to her, his sleek power that responded so swiftly to the gentle touch of her hand.

"Ma'am," the doorman said, beckoning as the yellow cab slid into the curb.

She had almost reached it when from behind came a voice, smooth and smug. "Hello, Ms. Browning. Or should I say Ms. *Frensham?*"

She almost tripped; she could feel the color drain from her face, seeping back to her heart and taking all warmth and life with it.

Peter Sanderson stood there, his broad, ruddy face suffused with a satisfaction that sent chills as far as her feet.

"You coming, lady?" the cabdriver yelled indignantly.

For once grateful for the legendary impatience of New York cabbies, she collapsed into the car, but the man who must have dug and dug until he found his bit of dirt followed her in. Because she had time to realize that she needed to know exactly what he had discovered, she moved across the seat.

She did not bargain, however, on having him lean forward and give the address of a famous and extremely expensive restaurant to the driver.

"What—" she began to protest, only to be overridden.

"I think we need to talk," he said complacently, his intent eyes searching her face. "And we'll have some privacy there."

He was just as dangerous as Nicholas, but in a more alarming way. There was something not quite normal about Peter Sanderson, something that made her skin creep and her heart thump.

"I didn't expect to see you here," she said, striving to sound normal. Surprised, even a bit taken aback, but not in the least afraid.

He smiled. "Didn't you?"

"I gather you're in town for the conference," she said, her fingers curving tightly around the strap of her bag, keeping it between them like a kind of flimsy bulwark.

"Partly," he said significantly.

The cab pulled up. After paying the driver, Sanderson got out, taking her elbow in a grip that made her want to shrink instinctively away.

"I'm not dressed for this," she said, looking about.

His smile was patronizing. "My dear Mariel, you'll outshine most of the women in there, as I'm sure you're aware."

She curved her mouth in what she hoped didn't register as a parody of a smile. "Pull the other leg," she invited ironically.

"Come on, now, don't tell me you didn't know that all of us at Bride's Bay thought you were very pretty." His smile didn't match the malicious calculation in his eyes. "In fact, you made poor Susan quite jealous. She's accustomed to being the beauty of the delegation, and for a while there it looked as though Nicholas had found a redhead he liked just as much as he liked her. However, they're back together again now."

He didn't care who he hurt, Mariel realized, provided he could turn it to Nicholas's disadvantage. When he said the other man's name his voice had a slow, gloating intonation he couldn't hide.

She'd deal with the pain of that later; for the present there was a greater imperative. It would be utterly unfair if Nicholas had to suffer any consequences because her parents had been traitors to their country.

And it would, she thought with bitter irony, make her sacrifice pointless.

She drew a deep, carefully regimented breath. Exactly how much did Peter Sanderson know? Now that her first panic was over she knew that it was unlikely he'd found any evidence of their idyll on the island—Liz Jermain ran a tight ship when it came to security—because if he did have hard proof he wouldn't need to waylay her.

It was much more likely that he merely suspected an affair. So he was probably intending to probe her reactions and responses for indications of guilt; that remark about Nicholas and Susan being together again would have been thrown in to see if she considered herself a woman scorned.

A fierce indignation stiffened her spine. *Let's see, shall we,* she thought, *just how comprehensively and conclusively I can fool you.*

They were seated at a small discreet table with a good view of the entrance, and after a quite unnecessary fuss over the right wine, during which her companion showed a rather cursory knowledge of the subject, she ordered an appetizer and a salad.

"That doesn't seem much," Peter Sanderson observed, an odd gleam in his eye. "Aren't you feeling well? You look as though you've lost some weight since we were on the island."

Did he think she'd been wasting away from a broken heart? "Summer always does that to me. I'm not a big eater," she said, "and they do big meals here."

"Ah, you've been here before?" He didn't manage to hide a flash of chagrin.

What a strange man he was. "No, never. I was talking generally. Most restaurants in America have huge servings."

But he was looking past her with that gloating look once more. Even as he said, "Well, well, well, look who's here," she knew just what he had done.

He'd set her up. Of course he hadn't just brought her here to pump her. He was cleverer than she had thought; he had decided to see for himself just how close Nicholas and she were. *Please,* she had time to pray, *not Susan, too.*

CHAPTER EIGHT

AT LEAST SHE HAD her back to the entrance, so as Peter Sanderson got to his feet and waved, Mariel had a precious few seconds to drag her tattered composure about her.

But as Sanderson's gaze moved avidly to her face, she realized she was not to be spared anything. For it was Susan's voice she heard, the higher, feminine tones carrying across the room.

"It's bizarre," she was saying. Her voice dropped, but was still only too audible. "Did you know they were going to be here?"

"No," Nicholas said coolly.

Attack, Mariel ordered herself. *That way you don't have to defend yourself. Think of this whole ghastly situation as a play,* she commanded that shrinking, terrified inner part of her, the lonely, frightened child who wanted to race out of the restaurant and cower in her apartment until they'd all left New York.

"You and the rest of the New Zealand delegation seem to have similar tastes in food," she said dryly to her tormenter, relieved to hear that her voice obeyed her will.

She allowed herself to turn slightly and smile at Susan and Nicholas with the right amount of surprise, of pleasure, that a casual meeting like this should engender.

Of course Nicholas's face revealed nothing. He would have made a magnificent gambler. She could visualize him in some Regency gaming hell, not a flicker of expression warming the hard, handsome face as he negligently won thousands of pounds.

"Hello, Mariel," he said, nodding, his eyes the cold pale green of glacier ice.

Susan's smile was coated with reserve. "Hello, Mariel. Fancy seeing you here."

"I must admit it's not one of my usual haunts," Mariel explained. "If I hadn't more or less been kidnapped by Peter, I wouldn't be here tonight. Restaurants like this are for out-of-towners—New Yorkers pride themselves on living on car exhaust and adrenaline."

It was as much of a warning as she dared give Nicholas, and she couldn't risk even a fleeting glance to see whether it had been understood.

"That's coming it a bit strong," Peter said, beaming expansively. "I saw her as she came out of the Cosmopolitan and talked her into dining with me."

Hoping that Nicholas would see and understand, Mariel gave a small, incredulous smile.

Susan slipped her hand into the crook of Nicholas's arm. "What fun for you both," she said, her gaze traveling from Mariel's face to Peter's. "How are you, Mariel?"

"Join us and find out properly," Peter said, playing the effusive host rather badly. "No, I mean it—we'll have a little reunion!"

He signaled the waiter, but even as the man came up Nicholas said deliberately, "I'm sorry, but Susan and I are having a working dinner. We must get together some other time."

And he and Susan—the latter throwing a swift, enigmatic glance at Mariel—followed the waiter to another table across the room.

Calling on all her reserves of strength, Mariel said calmly, "So now, Peter, tell me why you've been digging around in my life. I consider it to be an invasion of privacy, and you'd better have a damned good reason for doing it."

He had hidden his anger and frustration remarkably well, but such open provocation brought color to his skin and a harsh note to his voice. "I consider it a matter of security."

"Really?" She didn't attempt to hide her disbelief. "And exactly what threat do I represent to New Zealand's security?"

He paused until the waiter had placed the appetizers in front of them. Carefully keeping her eyes from the dark head on the other side of the room, Mariel picked up her spoon and forced herself to eat clam chowder.

"I wasn't happy with the hotel's security check," he said stiffly, "so I ran my own, and that turned up a couple of intriguing facts, enough to send me looking for connections. I found it very interesting." He spun the words out, glancing sideways at her, and when she merely looked inquiringly at him, repeated them as a taunt. "Yes, *very* interesting that a daughter of New Zealand's two most notorious traitors should be working in such a sensitive area."

"You suspect me of selling secrets to the Russians?" she asked with smooth sarcasm.

"No, but there is such a thing as industrial espionage," he asserted, watching her with an intensity in which she could read anger and bafflement.

"So you assume that treachery is genetic. I see." She swallowed a small amount of the white wine he'd ordered and asked sweetly, "And did you find any signs of industrial espionage in my dossier?"

"No," he snapped.

"Then perhaps you'd like to tell me what all this is about?"

It was a bold request, but she felt strong enough to push it.

He shrugged. "Nothing. I just thought I should tell you that I'd been prowling amongst your records," he said, and if she hadn't overheard his impassioned diatribe against

Nicholas on the golf course at Bride's Bay she might have believed him.

"Thank you," she said, adding, "I think."

He nodded across the room, saying with a sly smile, "That doesn't look like a business meeting, does it?"

Mariel looked. Susan was laughing, her eyes fixed on Nicholas's dark face as though all her hopes for the future rested there.

"No," Mariel said, marveling at her ability to sound confident and unconcerned when her whole being was racked by a soul-deep cry of outrage and misery. The only thing that consoled her was that Peter Sanderson wouldn't be learning anything from this expensive exercise. "But what has that to do with the fact that you've been invading my privacy and threatening me?"

"I did not threaten you," he blustered.

"Then what do you call referring to me by a name I've long given up and hijacking my cab? Why do you think I'm here, Mr. Sanderson? You said that we needed to talk. Believe me, from my position that sounded like a threat."

He glowered at her with dislike. "Well, you were wrong." And as though he couldn't bear not to keep an eye on Nicholas, his gaze slid sideways again. "Rude bastard," he said, adding with a quick suppression of his emotions, "I imagine there'll be an engagement announcement before long."

Calling on every reserve of power and self-control she possessed, Mariel said evenly, "I'm very pleased for them."

He said acidly, "They deserve each other. Stuck-up bitch."

His eyes lingered on Susan's face. The other woman chose that moment to laugh and touch Nicholas's mouth with her long forefinger, and a spasm of pain shot through Mariel, echoed by the look in Peter Sanderson's eyes.

Join the club, she felt like saying, and experienced a jolt of sympathy. Now she understood why his dislike of Nicholas had turned the perilous corner into obsessive hatred. He was in love with Susan, and seeing her with Nicholas must rub raw the inferiority complex that bedeviled him.

She said, "I think at the very least you owe me an apology."

Sanderson peered at her, obviously trying to assess her mood. To stop any further speculation she played a hunch and said, "I assume your superiors don't know anything about your extracurricular activities."

"Of course they do," he said promptly.

She nodded. "Then I intend to write to them registering my anger and asking them how New Zealand's privacy laws deal with this sort of thing. I'm still a citizen."

With bland obduracy she met and parried a glare compounded of rage and frustration intermingled, she was glad to see, with alarm.

"Of course," she continued delicately, "if I could be sure that this information is not going to be bandied about, I might be persuaded to forget about your prying. Knowledge of my parents' treachery is not going to harm me in any way, but I prefer not to talk about it."

He understood. He said with great dignity, "I assure you, it will remain completely secret."

"Good," she said, not believing a word of it. Oh, he'd keep quiet for the present, but if he ever saw a chance of using the information to advance his career, he'd do it.

Still, she could deal with that if and when it ever happened. "Then as long as it stays secret I won't need to contact anyone," she said calmly, and began to talk of something else.

To her great relief, he followed suit; apparently he had decided there was nothing to be gained from probing. She and Nicholas had managed to appear like acquaintances, nothing more. Afterward, when she was safely at home, she tried to recall what they had spoken of. A vain attempt, for all she could remember was the pain Nicholas's presence with Susan had caused her, the intense emotional agony she'd been forced to push deep beneath her conscious mind.

As she walked out of the restaurant with Peter Sanderson, he said, "I'll take you home."

"No, thank you, that's not necessary," she said.

A dull flush darkened his face. "Why so fussy?" he sneered. "You let bloody Leigh kiss you a couple of nights after you met him."

So that was why he'd been so convinced there was something between them.

Although her skin crawled at the thought of being watched by this man, she said steadily, "I see your spying is not confined to raking through old documents. Well, to convince you I'm not a slut, I'll tell you how that happened. Your research will, no doubt, have told you that a couple of years ago I was in love with an English diplomat."

"Yes," he muttered. "You dumped him."

Not for the world was she going to correct him. "Nicholas reminded me a bit of him," she said clearly. "But one thing I've learned is that you can't let the past shadow the future, and that it's no use raking over old embers. Both Nicholas and I realized I was letting my memories take over. And now, if you don't mind, I'm going home."

It seemed he believed her. He said, "Yes, well, I see. I'm sorry."

"Your apology is accepted," she returned frigidly.

At home she sat for some time in the small living room, then got up and drew a glass of water, drinking it down without, for once, wrinkling her nose at the flat, insipid warmth of it.

She had to get away. She couldn't bear the thought of running into Nicholas again, especially not with Susan. She lifted the hot weight of her hair away from her neck and listened to the traffic's dull, never-ending roar.

The telephone shrilled suddenly, making her jump. Staring at it, she willed it to stop, but it kept going and in the end, knowing who it was, she picked it up and said wearily, "Hello."

"What the hell was that all about?"

A humorless smile stretched her mouth. "He told me he'd done some research and found out who my parents were."

"Damn his hide. I'll see to it that he pays for his snooping," Nicholas said.

"He saw us kissing on the island and decided to dig into my past. He's paranoid, Nicholas. He's also in love with Susan." Hearing an intake of breath at the other end of the line, she hurried on, "That's part of the reason he hates you, and I'm afraid it *is* hatred. I'd watch him very carefully if I were you. When he discovered who my parents were, he was sure he'd be able to use the information to discredit you in some way."

"Does he know we were on the island together?" he asked brusquely.

"No, I'm certain he doesn't." She steadied her voice with nothing but raw, steely willpower. "He's suspicious, but that's all. Otherwise, why would he have arranged that elaborate charade tonight? He hoped we'd betray something if he sprang me on you."

"You're probably right." Nicholas's voice was completely noncommittal.

The sooner this was over the sooner he'd hang up. "You're quite safe, Nicholas," she said quickly.

"And what about you? I'll bet he's already thinking of ways to use this information against you."

"I doubt it. I threatened to go to his superiors if I ever heard the slightest whisper, and he didn't seem to like the idea of that."

"No, I don't suppose he did." Nicholas paused, then said, "Mariel—"

"So you don't need to worry at all," she interrupted, listening to her heart break. "Thanks for ringing. Goodbye."

And replacing the receiver she sat quietly, looking at nothing with burning eyes.

A friend had a cabin in the woods of New Brunswick. She had her own key, and she toyed with the idea of catching a flight to Saint John and spending a week there. Then, the trade conference over, it would be safe to come back to New York.

But she couldn't do it. She'd be letting Carole down, and besides, who was she fooling? Nicholas wouldn't come looking for her, not even to explain anything. She had given up any rights when she refused to marry him.

TEN DAYS LATER she was closing the street door behind her, her mind set on grocery shopping, when a clipped voice said, "Mariel?"

Mariel jumped. She recognized that voice, although it was not the one for which she listened unconsciously every moment of every day.

Slowly she turned. David St. Clair stood there, handsome face smiling, blue eyes serious beneath his cap of golden hair. "Hello," she said, fighting a disappointment so acute it made her heartsick.

"Mariel," he repeated. "How are you?"

She withdrew slightly. "I'm fine. How are you?"

"Well, thank you." His eyes devoured her face. "You look a little tired," he said after an awkward moment. "Don't tell me that you've been kept up all night translating for importunate businessmen?"

"No," she said quietly. She had loved this man, made love with him, grieved for months after he left her, and now she wondered how on earth it had all happened. She felt nothing, not even a mild pleasure, nothing of the fear and anger and outrage and heartfelt longing that he'd caused her. What a waste of emotions.

Is that how it would be with Nicholas?

No.

David shot his cuff back to look at the thin gold watch that had been his grandfather's. "How about a cup of coffee?" he asked. "Does the deli across the way still make brilliant sandwiches? Remember how I used to pick you up on a Sunday morning and we'd buy sandwiches and go to Central Park for lunch under the trees? You only ever ate half of yours—you always fed the rest to the squirrels." His voice was intimate, coaxing and confident. "I think about those sandwiches quite often."

"The deli's changed hands and I don't want any coffee, thank you," she said coolly.

He gazed at her with possessive eyes. "I want to know how you are, Mariel. Come on, it won't take much time."

Once she would have followed him to the ends of the earth. Now it seemed too much trouble to cross the road with him. Damn Nicholas! He had imprinted himself so firmly on her that drinking coffee with another man seemed like the worst sort of faithlessness.

Revulsion at this realization persuaded her to look in turn at her watch. "All right, but I can only spend ten minutes. I'm on my way to the agency."

"Good." Automatically he took her elbow and escorted her into the deli. Once seated with their coffee in front of them, he said, "How are you really, my dear?"

What on earth did he expect her to say? *Fully recovered from the knowledge that although you loved me, you loved your career more?*

"I'm fine," she said, trying to sound cheerful and reserved at the same time. "Things are going really well. How are you?"

His smile was muted. "I'm in pretty good shape." Stirring a spoonful of sugar into his cup, he inhaled deeply and said, "Ah, this is wonderful. I wonder why Americans can't produce a decent pot of tea when they make the best coffee in the world. Do you ever think of us, Mariel?"

She almost spluttered into her drink, only just restraining herself, although not before she'd burned her tongue. "No," she said cautiously, putting down the cup. "Not often, anyway."

"I think about us all the time," he said, watching her with a wistfulness that didn't appear feigned.

She shrugged. "It seems a fruitless exercise, especially as you . . ." . . . *have a wife,* she'd been going to finish.

"I haven't been able to get you out of my head," he said, searching her face with a hot blue gaze.

"Raking up the past is another fruitless exercise," she said briskly. "It's over and done with. What are you doing in New York?" The trade conference had finished three days ago, so it couldn't be that.

"Work—the meeting of the General Assembly," he said indifferently. "I'll be here a couple of weeks. Look, why don't we get together some night?"

She didn't even have to think. "It wouldn't be wise," she said, putting her untouched cup back on the saucer. "You're married, David."

"Oh, God," he said, looking at her wearily. "And what a farce that is! I should never have let you go, Mariel. Never have let anything but us matter. I felt I owed loyalty to my family, to my...oh, to everyone who wanted me to do well, I suppose, and your parents certainly would have been a rather murky splotch on my record. But honestly, darling, since we broke up nothing has gone right for me. I almost had a breakdown, you know. I had to take several months off."

No wonder Nicholas had accused her of ruining his career. Because David seemed to need a response, she said, "I didn't know. Are you all right now?"

Not touching her, he leaned forward, his face intently earnest, his glance a mixture of pleading and need. "Oh, yes, I got over it. Physically, anyway. But...Mariel, it hurts to breathe when you're not with me. What really hurts, though, what I can't ever forget, is that I deserve to be unhappy," he said deeply. "I was a coward. I let the best thing in my life slip away because I didn't have the guts to make a stand against all the expectations everyone piled on me."

She had no idea what to say to this. Six months ago she might have understood, even been secretly thrilled by his confession, so patently sincere, but now she felt nothing but distaste. Nicholas had stormed the guarded castle of her heart and thrown out its previous inhabitant, banishing his image so successfully that her love for David was a dim, insubstantial wraith from a previous existence.

He said, "We didn't meet accidentally. I've been waiting for you."

She had never loved him, Mariel thought with the shock of a simple clarion call of realization.

She said politely, "I'm sorry. Even if I still felt the same way about you—and I don't—I never go out with married men."

"Darling," he said, clearly shaken. "Mariel...Mariel, my marriage means nothing to either of us. Cosima married me because she thought it was time to settle down and I was suitable, and I married her for exactly the same reasons, also because I didn't care who I married if I couldn't have you. My parents thought she was an excellent catch—the daughter of an earl, you know." In spite of everything he couldn't hide a note of pride.

"I'm sorry," she said, attempting to conceal her aversion, "but although you might not have loved each other, I'm sure you both vowed to be loyal."

His face contorted. "I've made my bed," he said on a note of regret and bitterness, "and now I should lie in it, is that it?"

Gently she said, "I wish you all the best, David."

"So you've found someone else. I was sure you would, but I had to try." He got to his feet, looking down at her with greedy despair in his eyes. "You deserve someone who will fight for you," he said. "I hope you'll be very happy, Mariel."

And he bent and kissed her lightly on her startled lips and went out into the street.

STUDENTS WERE BACK in school, and the number of tourists on the streets diminished slightly. Mariel kept her emotions at bay with hard work and long hours.

"Saving up for a holiday?" Carole asked.

Only then accepting a decision made a long time ago, Mariel nodded.

"Where?"

She felt self-conscious, even a bit stupid, but she said, "I thought I'd go back to New Zealand and see what difference the last ten years have made."

With a New Yorker's inherent arrogance Carole said, "What is there to do in New Zealand? Look at scenery?"

"Mainly." It was time to face demons. She'd go back to the little town where she'd been so unhappy and look up a few people—especially, she thought, the neighbor who'd been so kind to her. When she'd left New Zealand she'd kept in touch with Mrs. Reilly, still sent her postcards and Christmas cards, but that was all. "I haven't really seen much of the place."

"When do you plan to go?"

Mariel smiled. "February. It'll be summer there then, so I'll come back with a tan."

"You can get one of those in the Caribbean and it won't cost you so much."

Mariel laughed. "My parents didn't come from the Caribbean."

"Oh, well, if you're going back to your roots, I suppose you'll have to get it out of your system," Carole said, nodding wisely. "By the way, I got a call yesterday from that island resort—Bride's Bay—in South Carolina. They wanted you in a couple of weeks' time."

Mariel hadn't told the agency that she wouldn't accept bookings from that hotel anymore, and she was glad she could say casually, "I'm in Chicago then, aren't I?"

"Yeah, well, I suggested Karen to Bride's Bay and they okayed it, but I've just got a fax canceling."

"Another high-powered meeting gone phut," Mariel said with an inward shudder.

The last thing she wanted to do was return to the island. In fact, sometimes she wondered whether the almost involuntary decision to return to New Zealand had been based on a desire to put as much distance as possible between her and the place where she and Nicholas had loved so sweetly, with such fire and tenderness and intense, consuming passion that even now, all these months later, her dreams were heated by memories and images.

The meeting with David had brought insights and a sense of closure, of final parting, but Nicholas's dark strength and dominance had already banished David from her mind and heart. She would never see Nicholas again, unless an unkind fate threw them together coincidentally, but she'd given up hoping that she would get over him as she had David.

Oh, no doubt there'd come a time when she'd be able to think of him without this searing pain, but she would always love him. He had made himself master of her heart.

ONE MONTH TO THE DAY after the meeting with David, Mariel arrived home from an exhausting international seminar involving hours of simultaneous interpretation and was pouring herself a glass of iced tea when the phone rang. Yawning with exhaustion, although her mind was buzzing, she picked up the receiver.

"You're wanted at Bride's Bay this weekend," Carole informed her cheerfully. "I've done some juggling because they were really insistent that you go—you must have good relations with the boss down there! The usual agreement—leave tomorrow on the 7 a.m. plane via Washington. Your ticket will be waiting at the counter.''

Mariel froze, but she knew she couldn't refuse. And who knew, she thought wearily, perhaps this would be some sort of exorcism. She would get it over and done with and then she wouldn't ever have to fear it again. And as she had no intention of going anywhere near the cottages, she wouldn't be faced with that particular agony.

AT THE AIRPORT in Charleston the resort's helicopter was waiting. "I've just dropped off a couple of guests," the pilot, a tall, rugged man with a face too cynical to be handsome said in answer to her query. "Ms. Jermain said I might as well bring you back.''

Although she liked going on the ferry, Mariel contrived to look grateful. "That's nice of her," she said.

He shrugged. "She's a nice woman," he said deliberately, swinging Mariel's case into the chopper before helping her in.

And the pilot was a nice man, she thought as the helicopter rose from the ground and swerved across the complicated intermingling of sea and marsh and land that was South Carolina's coastal area. She didn't know him well; hotel staff said he was something of a dark horse, but he'd always been pleasant to her. Perhaps she should forget Nicholas and concentrate on him.

She was seized with a tide of revulsion so intense that it kept her silent all the way to the island. If only life were that simple!

Half an hour later she was once more back in the business center talking to Elise. "How are things going?''

Elise smiled. "Better," she said. "Jimmy now has some faint inkling of what he did to Caitlin. Oh, we aren't going to get back together, and I don't think he's ever going to stop being a selfish, thoughtless adolescent, but at least he's handed over enough money so that I can buy a house in the village, and he's admitted that Caitlin's probably better off with me for the moment.''

"And Caitlin?''

"She likes living in the village. Now that Jimmy's stopped his campaign to steal her away, she's beginning to settle down. They talk on the phone every week, and we're flying out to spend some of next summer with him.'' She looked quizzically at Mariel. "Jimmy was very impressed by the man who knocked him out. Angry, but impressed. He's used to being the biggest, toughest, most macho man around, and Mr. Leigh's finishing him off so easily really astonished him. Do you see anything of him now?''

"No,'' Mariel said, quickly adding, "I'm glad things have worked out for you.''

"Life's certainly much better than it was before.'' Frowning, Elise looked down at her desk. "Oh, I have a message for you from Liz Jermain. She wants to see you in her office as soon as you can get there.''

"Okay, I'll be back later and you can fill me in on what I'm to do.''

Mariel strode to the manager's office, testing her mental pulse. Unhappiness—yes, she was unhappy, but she was accustomed to that now. For the rest, well, she didn't feel too bad.

Perhaps this minor ceremony of exorcism was going to work.

Liz Jermain was coming out of her office as Mariel approached. "Oh, hello,'' she said after a keen, intent glance. "I'm sorry, something's just come up—I shouldn't be long. Just go in and wait, will you?''

"Of course.''

Mariel turned the handle, opened the door and walked in.

And in one shattering moment her previous confidence stood revealed for the bravado it was. Because Nicholas was there, waiting for her.

Blindly she took a step backward, her pupils dilating endlessly as her hand groped behind her for the handle.

"No," he said with uncompromising authority, "this time you're not going to run away or force me to go."

In a voice she didn't recognize she blurted out the first thing that came to mind. "Was that you—when I couldn't come last time?" she asked.

"Yes." His eyes narrowed. "I went to quite a lot of trouble to get you down here, and I was angry when you chickened out."

"I did not chicken out." It seemed important to tell him this, even though she knew she was using it as a distancing tactic while she struggled to deal with the intense emotions roused by his presence. "I had a prior booking, damn you!"

Without much interest, he said, "Did you? Ah, well, it doesn't matter much. You're here now. It took me considerable persuasion to talk Ms. Jermain into allowing me to use the hotel to get you here, and then I had to do it all over again. Even now she's not entirely sure that she's doing the right thing." He sounded quite casual.

If he's like David, wanting to take up where we left off, what will I do?

I'll die.

"Come away from the door," he said. "She's trying to get in."

Stiffly, keeping her face so rigid it felt wooden, Mariel moved into the office as the door opened behind her.

He didn't look any different, she thought, trying not to stare, trying desperately to summon a cool composure and failing miserably.

His face almost quizzical, his eyes giving nothing away, he said, "Come in, Ms. Jermain. Mariel will tell you that she isn't being threatened—"

"I'd like her to tell me herself," Liz said crisply, with another intent look at Mariel.

Nicholas, damn him, looked amused.

Mariel said, "It's all right, Ms. Jermain. He's not a homicidal maniac or even," she added with a cutting snap to her voice, "particularly dangerous."

"Oh, yeah?" said the manager somewhat inelegantly. "Any man who could talk me into a stunt like this has to be dangerous. Do you want him here?"

"Yes," Mariel said, because she knew there was no way out of this meeting. Nicholas radiated a hard-edged vitality, a sense of purpose that exhausted her.

"Then perhaps we can let Ms. Jermain have her office back," Nicholas said with smooth urbanity. "I have a suite, or if you'd rather meet in neutral territory..."

"Your suite will be fine," Mariel said stiffly.

They went up to his suite in silence, walked without speaking along the corridor, and silently she went ahead of him through the door he held open.

"Sit down," he said. "I'll get you a drink. Mineral water?"

"Yes, thank you."

He brought it to her, waited while she drank half of it, and then said pleasantly, "Tell me what it was like living in New Zealand after your parents died."

Spluttering, she set the glass down on the table. "Why?"

"We have to start somewhere," he said. "I think it's relevant."

He'd never looked more determined, more relentless. She could feel the force of his will beating her resistance down. How could he do this to her? Was it just an egotistical man's anger at being refused?

Resentfully she flared, "Is this more of your pop psychology?"

"Stop trying to annoy me," he said blandly.

Biting her lip, she surrendered. After all, the sooner this was over the sooner he'd go. "I hated it," she said in a voice drained of energy and expression. "Somehow everyone knew who I was, even though my aunt had changed my name, and they tormented the life out of me. I was absurdly sensitive, which didn't help."

"And your aunt? How did she feel about looking after you?"

From the past came the voices, the children's taunts, her aunt's continual complaints: *If it wasn't for you I'd be where I should be, right at the top. You and your parents dragged me down...*

"She blamed me," Mariel said, shrugging. "Well, my parents mainly, but she couldn't tell them how she felt so she told me, instead."

"And every childhood misdemeanor was traced back to your parents' treachery, every character flaw seen as the start of the slippery fall to perdition and ruin."

He seemed to be quoting. She asked tiredly, "How do you know?"

"I went back and asked questions. A Mrs. Reilly told me you were the saddest child she'd ever seen."

Remembering the compassionate, always pleasant woman who used to talk to her whenever she got the chance, Mariel found her eyes filling with stupid tears. Swallowing, she said, "She was kind to me." And then in bewilderment, "Why did you go there? My childhood has nothing to do with you."

"I think it does," he said quietly. "For years you've believed that what your parents did put you completely beyond the pale. Your aunt sounds like the last person who should've been given the care of a bright, confused, grief-stricken child. Thanks to her you grew up firmly convinced you weren't worthy of being loved. I'll bet any confidence you've managed to achieve is shackled to your work, your skills. Then you met David St. Clair and you let gratitude overwhelm your common sense."

"Gratitude?"

"What else was it, Mariel?" His voice was a cool challenge. "Besides physical attraction? You're far too intelligent to love a man who let outdated ideas of family loyalty and class dictate who he married—unless you were struggling with a sense of inferiority, of being unlovable. You admired him, but above all you were grateful to him for loving you."

Gratitude? Biting back a protest, she forced herself to consider his statement. Had she such low self-respect that she was *grateful* to a man for wanting her? Dazed with happiness, for a short while she had juggled a fragile bubble of hope, a bubble that had shattered when she told David who she was and he had rejected her. A woman with healthy self-esteem would have been angry at his rejection; she had accepted it without demur. Indeed some part of her, too deep to be accessible to her conscious mind, had expected it all along.

With enormous, resentful reluctance she admitted that Nicholas's theory made sense. A basic lack of faith in herself would explain why she had let David—and Nicholas—go out of her life without a battle.

She stared out the window, toward the trees in the far distance. Somewhere there, sandwiched between the woods and the sea, was the cottage where they had spent their idyll.

Nicholas had been right when he'd insisted she felt far more than the simple, direct urgings of lust. They shared the same sense of humor; his ice-clear brain had sparked off hers, and they had both enjoyed the discussions that sometimes became heated, but never degenerated into arguments.

And it would be foolish to decry the sex. When he'd made love to her Nicholas hadn't been like David, careful to ensure she had reached her peak before he succumbed to his own pleasure. There had been nothing careful about Nicholas. The consuming, white-hot strength of his desire had swept her into a realm she'd never reached before.

In Nicholas's arms she had found a different Mariel, a woman who had no inhibitions, who had been warm and earthy and eagerly erotic, a woman who valued herself. They had come together as equals, a man and a woman whose passions were complementary. That, she thought painfully, had been one of the reasons she had turned tail. That sensuous, uninhibited aspect of her personality frightened her.

And when Nicholas left her he had ripped her heart out, not merely bruised it.

"What is all this in aid of?" she asked aggressively.

"Do you agree with me so far?"

"Yes, I suppose so," she said. She couldn't bear to look at him in case she saw nothing of what she wanted in his face, so she stared down at her hands. "Nicholas, why did you go to all this trouble? What is this all about?"

"Can't you guess?"

CHAPTER NINE

SHE SHOOK HER HEAD. Was he trying to persuade her to marry him? If so, she'd have to stand firm against the pleadings of her heart, because all the insights in the world into her own psyche were not going to persuade her to wreck his career.

She clasped her hands at the back of her neck, tipping her head into her laced fingers, stretching the taut muscles there as she grimaced.

I've wanted to be a diplomat ever since I was twelve. His words echoed in her brain.

Even though she'd found paradise in his arms, even though he'd asked her to marry him, she couldn't do it. Love had responsibilities. He was innocent of anything but wanting her. Her aunt had also been innocent, but her affection for her sister and brother-in-law had turned to hatred over the years, and Mariel couldn't bear it if one day Nicholas looked at her with the same mixture of blame and loathing.

"I want you to come and meet someone," he said calmly.

"Meet someone? Who?"

"His name won't mean anything to you. Come on."

"I need to change—"

One of his rare smiles eased the hard contours of his face. "You're fine just the way you are," he said.

Noting the uncompromising look in his eyes, she got up, in her heart the old futile yearning that somehow things could be changed, that her parents had thought for a moment before they embarked on their career as traitors, that the sins of the fathers were not visited on the children.

"And then you'll leave me alone?" she asked abruptly.

His smile became twisted. "If you want me to."

After a short walk along the corridor he knocked at a door; a voice answered in a language she recognized as Russian.

Nicholas said in English, "Here she is," and the door opened, she concluded, after the unknown man behind it had sufficient time to consult the peephole.

He was short and bald, with shrewd dark eyes, high Slavic cheekbones and the solid build of a man who had once been all muscle. "Come in," he said in heavily accented English.

Totally bewildered, Mariel allowed herself to be ushered in; Nicholas kept his hand between her shoulder blades, the warmth of his palm burning through her dress. "This is Arkady Svetlanko," he said formally. "Mr. Svetlanko, this is Mariel Browning, who was born Mariel Frensham. You knew her parents in Hong Kong, I believe?"

If he'd held a knife to her throat, Mariel could not have been angrier or more shocked. But the Russian was thrusting out his hand, and the manners her mother had drummed into her stopped her from doing more than lance a glare at Nicholas as she obeyed the summons.

"Mr. Svetlanko," she said. "How do you do."

He had a firm, warm handshake, and there was something like sympathy in his dark eyes as he looked at her. "You see me as the enemy," he said. "For years I saw you as such, too. It seems foolish now, such a waste, and yet we were sure, all of us, that the future of the world depended on our machinations."

His remarks caught her attention; she looked at him properly, seeing strength of character and resolution in his features. "I suppose it did," she said a little uncertainly.

"Well, no doubt we will pay in some way for the things we did." He sounded as though he meant it. "My friend Nicholas Leigh tells me that you think your parents spied for the Soviets while they were in Hong Kong."

She couldn't look at Nicholas, although she could feel him behind her as a bulwark, both bodyguard and warden. "It's long past," she said. "As you said, it doesn't matter now."

"I think that it does," he said unexpectedly in his correct English. "And so does Mr. Leigh, or he would not have spirited me out of Moscow and brought me all the way to America simply to tell you that they did not spy for us. They were framed, I am afraid, and killed because they knew too much."

The room wavered in front of her. She drew in a jagged breath as Nicholas's hands closed on her upper arms and he said angrily, "You didn't need to be quite so brutal."

The Russian sounded weary. "There is no way to break such news gently," he said.

Nicholas guided her to a chair and sat her down. He didn't move away but stood behind her with one hand on her shoulder. Electricity surged from his fingers, a powerful current of feeling that was intensely protective.

"I'm all right," she said, steadying her voice with an effort. "How do you know this, Mr. Svetlanko?"

"It was my business to discover such things." He paused, his eyes moving from Mariel's taut face to that of the man behind her. "Your father had learned that there was a thriving trade in smuggled antiquities from China. He came across it because one of his interests was Chinese porcelain of the Ming dynasty. You have his collection, I presume?"

"No," she said numbly. "I don't know what happened to it."

"That is a pity. It was very good. He had a feel for porcelain, a natural instinct for what was fake and what was genuine. This was almost certainly his downfall. He noticed that more and more genuine porcelain was coming onto the market in Hong Kong, more than was known to be in the Western world. And once he started to ask questions he found other objects—priceless antiques such as bronzes and silk paintings, unique artifacts from burial sites—all national treasures. Of course he informed his superiors, and of course he was told not to do anything about it, that such things were not in his area of influence. But your father was a persistent man. He kept digging away, and eventually his activities came to the knowledge of the powerful Chinese tong that was doing the stealing and the selling. This business was very profitable for them. I am sure you are aware that there are in the world many unscrupulous millionaires who fancy themselves as connoisseurs. The tong decided to get rid of your father."

"So they had him framed," she said quietly. "Why did they choose to implicate the Soviets?"

"They certainly did not want anyone connecting the deaths to China," he said. "Russia was the logical nation to choose at the time."

"Why such an elaborate charade? Why didn't they just kill them?"

"Think, Ms. Browning." The Russian spoke didactically, as though this were a classroom lesson. "They wanted no hint of the market in antiquities to escape—the Chinese government would not have stood idly by and let their birthright bleed through their fingers. Besides, at least one important official in China was conniving at this trade, a man who would have lost his life if it was discovered. It was a reasonably simple matter to cast suspicion on your parents and then to kill them and make it seem like a suicide pact. They also made sure that the names of several agents were supplied to me. The deaths of those men added verisimilitude to the scenario the tong concocted."

Tears ached at the back of Mariel's eyes. She said huskily, "Why didn't they kill me, too? I was in the bedroom asleep when it happened."

"They were professional," the Russian said, not without compassion. "There was no need to kill you. You knew nothing."

"And did they arrange for the maid to find them?" she asked. Nicholas's fingers tightened on her shoulder.

Svetlanko said, "She did as she was told. Apparently it was felt that your parents were so devoted that they would not have risked the possibility of your discovering them."

Nicholas said, "It's over, Mariel. Your parents are dead, but at least they were not traitors."

She should be feeling wonderful. But she felt only anguish at the tragedy of it all, the shattered lives—her parents', her aunt's—the misery of those childhood years, the useless lies and treachery and deaths. She looked at the Russian. "How do you know all this?"

"I made it my business to find out. After all, they were supposed to be spying for us and I knew they were not."

She nodded. "You were right, Mr. Svetlanko, it all does seem a waste now," she said desolately.

"I am sorry," the man said. "There is much that cannot be righted, many wrongs that are written in the history books as truths. But at least your friend Nicholas Leigh has made this right for you."

Mariel got to her feet. Her bones were filled with lead, she thought distantly. But she stood straight-backed and smiled at the Russian and said, "Thank you for doing this."

He laughed and looked at Nicholas. "Do not thank me. I am a pragmatist—I do not try to face down the whirlwind. Mr. Leigh is a force of nature when he wants something done." The dark eyes twinkled. "And this he wanted done very much. I am glad to have met you, Ms. Browning. Your father was a gallant gentleman, and your mother was warm and gracious and funny. I liked them both."

She swallowed, her memories at last robbed of bitterness. "Thank you," she said softly. "I will never be able to repay you."

He smiled, looking shrewdly from her face to that of the man who had tracked him down. "Repay Mr. Leigh," he said. "He has done all the work, not I."

"There's no question of repayment," Nicholas said with cool hauteur, holding out his hand.

Mariel watched them shake hands, the older man solid, almost squat against Nicholas's rangy elegance. She supposed she said goodbye; afterward she had no recollection of it. As she walked numbly back to Nicholas's suite she saw nothing of the charm and tasteful luxury that was the resort's trademark. In her mind raged the turmoil of Hong Kong, busy and noisy and packed with people, an image that was soon replaced by a wilder shore on the furthermost reaches of the Pacific, where an endless sea broke on abrupt little islands that sheltered golden beaches and rocky headlands and a green, untamed country.

"I'll order tea," Nicholas said when they were back in his suite. "Or would you rather have something stronger?"

"No, tea will be fine," she said colorlessly.

She heard his voice in the distance as she summoned memories of her parents, childhood ones untarnished by her aunt's bitterness, and she began to weep, the tears of a lifetime melting pain and anger and frustration, washing away the malign legacy of her parents' guilt.

And then she was surrounded by the warmth of his arms, supported by his lean body as he pulled her close and held her, his cheek on the top of her head.

After a while he said, "All right, that's enough. You're going to make yourself sick if you cry anymore."

"Bully," she said on a laborious, indrawn breath.

"Only when necessary." He held her away, pulling her hands down as she tried to cover her face. "At least," he said mockingly, "you'll never be able to say that the only reason I love you is because you're beautiful. At the moment you look like the wrath of God, and I find myself loving you more than ever. The tea will be here soon."

"It sounds wonderful," she said, suddenly shy. She searched his face, but the brilliant green-gold eyes gave nothing away. No tenderness softened their glitter, and yet he had said he loved her, and he had gone to incredible lengths to prove it—traveling all the way to New Zealand and Russia, bringing Arkady Svetlanko here.

"I need to wash my face," she said. As well, she needed time to herself.

He smiled. "All right."

She did look like the wrath of God, with swollen, red eyelids and a nose glowing like a beacon. Soggy and self-indulgent, she thought with a grimace as she turned on the faucet. And the splash of frigid water didn't help much. However, the icy shock of it did stop the slow welling of tears.

Of course her parents' vindication wasn't going to make any difference. She doubted whether Mr. Svetlanko would tell the world what had happened, so Nicholas's career would still be jeopardized by her past, but oh, she loved him so for doing this.

After blowing her nose heartily she walked back into the room. The tea tray was already there. For a moment she thought Nicholas had left, but he was standing by the window, looking down at the gardens. The instant he heard her he turned and scrutinized her thoroughly.

"That's slightly better," he observed, his mouth lifting at the corners.

"Don't flatter me."

His brows quirked. "I don't flatter anyone," he said dryly. "You should know that by now."

"An unlikely trait for a diplomat."

"I'm no longer a diplomat," he said casually—so casually that for a second she didn't comprehend the importance of his words.

When she did she gasped, "Oh, God, I was afraid of that—that's why I— Did Sanderson—"

"For heaven's sake, Mariel," he interrupted, "why must you think everything is your doing? It makes you sound utterly self-centered."

As no doubt he'd intended, his acerbic frankness jolted her out of the remorseful agitation his bombshell had caused. "Oh, does it?" she snapped, hackles rising. "Tell me why you decided to throw your career in, then."

"Pour me some tea and I will."

He waited until she'd done that, then hitched up a chair and sat down, long legs thrust out, his autocratic profile outlined against the heavy crimson curtains.

"I resigned because it came to a choice between diplomacy and you," he said, "and you won."

She said dully, "That was the choice I didn't want you to have to make."

"I know. You were being so insistent on self-sacrifice, going so bravely into martyrdom, that it didn't occur to you to ask me what I wanted."

"You've got a poisonous tongue," she retorted. "I didn't just—"

"No? Oh, I don't blame you. You were taught really well by that aunt of yours, who from all accounts was completely bitter and more than a little twisted. Her method of dealing with the situation couldn't have been worse."

"She did her best," Mariel objected. "She'd lost everything she cared for, her family, her career, her future—everything. Her life was ruined."

"Only in her estimation. The situation wasn't good, but she could have kept her job. She made the decision to leave."

Setting her cup down sharply, Mariel said with curt distinctness, "A request to resign doesn't leave you much choice in decisions."

"She wasn't asked to resign."

"How do you know?"

"I asked," he said calmly. "Something you didn't bother to do. She had you well and truly brainwashed. Tell me, why were you so worried about working with diplomats?"

She stared at him. "Because I knew my background would make people highly suspicious of me."

"Even after ten years of excellent work in a variety of fields, with never a breath of scandal or suspicion about you?" he asked conversationally. "Didn't it ever occur to you that you were overreacting to a ridiculous degree?"

"I...no," she said indignantly. "It's the way the game is played—you know that. Caesar's wife—and daughter—have to be above suspicion."

"And that stupid idiot who fell in love with you was too frightened to do anything about it without consulting his fossilized uncle, who still thinks that divorce is enough to keep you out of a decent university, let alone heaven," he retorted caustically. "Tell me, what did we do when we discovered who you were? Were you sacked? Sent back to New York in disgrace?"

"McCabe sent you off to woo information out of me!" she flared.

"I'll admit we were concerned, but that was simply a knee-jerk reaction. By the next morning we'd decided that your parents' treachery and death had nothing to do with you. You had an excellent record, and your reason for changing your name was understandable. Your fear, your conviction that you're marked with the mark of Cain, is irrational, Mariel."

"Not so irrational! You sneer at David," she retorted angrily, "but you left me, too."

He looked at her, his eyes half-closed, his mouth a straight, taut line. "You forget that I already knew who you were when I asked you to marry me. I left you at the cottage partly because I was furious that you lumped me in with St. Clair, but also because I could see you were convinced you were a liability—if not the kiss of death—to any diplomat. I realized you weren't ever going to change your mind. You wouldn't listen to me. You wouldn't even entertain the possibility that you might be wrong. I realized something else, too. Until then I'd managed to convince myself that although I wanted you and liked you and admired you, I didn't actually love you, not 'to the depth and breadth and height my soul can reach.' "

Tears welled in her eyes as she recognized the quotation. When she tried to answer, the words tangled on her tongue; blinking rapidly, she fought for composure.

His smile was lopsided. "Well, your refusal put paid to such arrogance. The prospect of living without you made my heart quail. I had to go, otherwise I'd have been reduced to begging."

Her heart turned over in her breast. "Don't be silly," she said uncertainly.

"You could make me do it," he said almost casually, as though it was a truth he'd long accepted. "After I'd got over my anger and, yes, and the hurt—" he smiled derisively "—I decided to find out exactly what made you so intransigent. To do that I had to go back to New Zealand."

She couldn't look at him. "My aunt did have reason to be bitter, Nicholas. Apart from anything else, she had me dumped on her."

"A situation she could have coped with. However, she resigned and disappeared, then set about punishing you for your parents' supposed sins by making sure you were as marked by the events as she'd allowed herself to be. She could have fought, Mariel. Instead, she ran away."

And he would think that the greatest sin. "I don't think she was deliberately cruel. People *were* awful to her," Mariel protested, trying to be objective.

He said grimly, "She might not have deliberately set out to ruin your life, but she certainly made you the scapegoat. As well as taking you to live in a small country town where everyone would know immediately who you were, she be-

haved like the Witch of Endor so that the conservative people there viewed her with grave suspicion. Then she made
their natural reactions her reason for cutting off all communication with them and retreating into an isolated ec-
centricity. No wonder you were desperate to leave New
Zealand. No wonder you never want to go back.''

Mariel bit her lip and picked up her cup. "I am going
back," she said. "I've booked my tickets for February."

"Have you indeed? Why, when you hate the place?"

"I don't! Oh, all right, my memories of New Zealand are
not exactly glowing ones, but I know that all New Zealanders are not small-minded bigots. I've met some charming
ones."

"What made you decide to go back?"

"Don't you ever give up?"

"Not when it's important for me," he said without mercy.

"I decided to go back because you love it," she muttered
crossly. "After I saw you in New York with Susan . . ." She
set her teacup down with a sharp click. "Just what were you
doing with her?" she asked fiercely. "You were at the Metropolitan Museum of Art. She stumbled as you were going
down the steps outside, and you put your arm around her
waist and kept it there until you were out of sight."

"Were you jealous?" he asked softly.

She hesitated, then shot him a defiant look. "I was eaten
up with it."

"Good." Straightening up, he smiled without humor.
"Now you have some small inkling of how I felt when you
compared me to David St. Clair."

"I didn't ever—"

"Oh, yes, you did. You compared us constantly. You even
expected me to reject you as he did. I won't tell you how
angry that made me—I thought, I love this woman with everything I have, everything I am, and she still thinks I'm
going to dump her because of what her parents did."

She protested, "I can't accept that my fears for your reputation were as irrational as you seem to think."

"Accept it," he said sternly.

She bit her lip. "But—"

"Don't start wallowing in guilt," he said, reading her reactions with merciless exactness. "If it's the last thing I do, I'll get you to admit that you don't carry the responsibility for the world on your shoulders. I was with Susan at the museum because there was an exhibition she wanted to see, and because she hoped she could talk me out of leaving the service. She failed. I wish I'd known you were there that day."

"I'm glad you didn't," she returned. "I was angry and—and desolate." Keeping her eyes on the florid Victorian pattern that embellished the china, she asked tentatively, "Nicholas, surely—the flaw in your argument that I'm being irrational is that you have left the service. And you wouldn't have done that if it hadn't been for me."

"I was already thinking of giving up foreign affairs when I met you."

She looked at him, trying to see past the handsome mask of his features to the cold, clear, incisive mind within. Could she believe him? Was he trying to make her feel better about his resignation? "Were you?"

"Mariel, I will never lie to you. Never. I know you have a lot of your life invested in that preposterous conviction, but it's wrong, implanted in your brain by a woman who was eaten up with a sense of bitter defeat." He didn't touch her, didn't even move, but she felt the powerful force of his will engulf her. His face was like stone, the only sign of life the leaping golden lights in his eyes. "You have to believe me," he said in a low, tense voice, "because if you don't, you will never trust me. And I need your trust, my darling."

Her pulse beat heavily in her throat. She felt herself being dragged into his gaze, drowning in green, experiencing the gold like sunlight from beneath water, and knew that just as he needed her faith she needed his honesty. With an instinct surer and more certain than the evidence of her senses she realized that she could give him what he wanted.

"I do trust you," she said in a low voice. The cup shook in her hand. She put it down in the saucer again and looked at him, her face transfigured. "I do, Nicholas. Truly."

His breath hissed through lips almost bloodless with the effort of waiting. "Thank God," he said. "I knew it would be hard—I didn't realize just how hard."

He took two strides across the room and pulled her into his arms, holding her so tightly clamped against him that she felt the urgent thunder of his heart driving into hers, the great strength unfettered for the first time.

"Darling," he said eventually in a muffled voice. "I've wanted you so many lonely hours—you've put me through hell! Never ever wonder whether I'm telling the truth. If I had to give up everything for you, I'd consider it all worthwhile."

"The world well lost for love," she murmured, really believing him for the first time, her heart incandescent with joy.

He picked her up and carried her to the sofa, then arranged them comfortably together, his arms around her, her head on his shoulder.

"Yes, because I've found a much better world, one with you at the center, in the core of my heart."

Shaken, she turned her face into his neck, listening to the soft thud of his heartbeat, breathing in the potent male scent that had haunted her for months.

"It's probably only fair to admit that, like you, I'm more influenced by my childhood than I'd realized." He spoke with a dry self-mockery that told her the insight had caused him more than a little disquiet. "In between checking out your childhood, tracking Svetlanko down and plotting to get you back, I've been doing a lot of thinking. When my father died he left me an obscene amount of money, half of which is in a family trust. The rest I set up in another trust, giving the trustees the brief that they were to use the income as venture capital to help people who want to make a difference, people with passion and ambition and intelligence who can't get money through the normal channels. I tried not to be involved, but over the years I've been drawn in. Slowly, almost without my realizing it, diplomacy has been losing its interest."

"Why?" she asked, unable to believe him.

He smiled ironically. "I've come to believe I chose it as a career because I wanted to distance myself from my father. I loved him, yet with the arrogance of youth I despised him, too. He was a brilliant man, strong and determined and dynamic. I don't know how old I was when I understood that my mother used her sexuality and her charm, her wit and intelligence, in a completely calculated manner, keeping him intrigued, playing on his emotions with all the skill of a major musical talent. Even having me was a career decision for her."

"Nicholas—"

"Mariel," he returned sardonically, and shrugged. "She told me so. She knew my father wouldn't divorce his wife, but because there were no children in the marriage, having his son would give her more power. I don't know how old I was when I decided I wasn't going to be like my father. No more than twelve, I think."

So he'd decided to become a diplomat.

"He must have loved her very much," she said.

"He loved what he thought she was—abjectly, besottedly, without reservations, without any self-defense. He would have given her the moon. Oh, she was clever. And she was surprisingly frank with me—she said I should know how women think."

Probably without realizing what she was doing, Nicholas's mother had corrupted him, destroyed some essential innocence before it even had time to form. No wonder he was cynical about women.

"Yes," he said, nodding as he saw the comprehension and the sympathy in her expression. "I grew up convinced that all women had their price, as irrational in my conviction as you were with yours. Then I met you. And suddenly I could see why my father gave his heart so utterly into a woman's keeping."

She shook her head. "No," she said unsteadily, "you couldn't have—"

"I looked at you," he interrupted relentlessly, "and my heart fell at your feet. I wanted you so much I could feel it like a drug in my veins. Within a few days I knew I'd do anything for you, kill for you, die for you—I fell in love at first sight. Of course I didn't concede the game, but perhaps you can understand how afraid I was when I acknowledged that nothing was ever going to be the same again. The whole basis I'd built my life on was shown to be a sham. It was a moment of bitter revelation."

"I don't believe in love at first sight," she said, her brow creasing. "Lust, yes, but love has to grow."

"That's what I thought it was to begin with," he agreed. "Simple lust—an honest, straightforward emotion, all about power and satisfaction. But by the time we left the resort I knew I had to have you, so I plotted quite cold-bloodedly to get you back there. I thought, I'll make sure she knows there's no future in it—that way I won't exploit her."

"Well, you did that all right," she said crossly, pulling away.

"After you spelled it out," he returned, coolly tucking her back against him, "that was when I had the first indication that things were not going to be so easy, because I was furious! I wanted you to protest, to demand more from me—and you were insultingly agreeable to an affair."

She didn't believe him until she tilted back her head and saw the truth in his eyes. "It hurt," she said slowly, "but I knew there couldn't be any future for us."

"I hated St. Clair." His voice was excoriating. "I'd only met the man a couple of times, didn't know anything about him beyond the fact that he had been your lover, but I hated him. Just another indication that I was in too far to be able to get out unscathed—an indication I ignored. But making love to you, being with you, was like finally reaching the doorstep of paradise. I already knew that you were gracious and calm and quick-witted, efficient and intelligent, that you had the compassion to help a woman when she was in trouble."

He paused for a breath, then went on, "Arrogantly, I thought I was safe behind my defenses, but you stole my heart so secretly that I never even bothered to look for it. I wanted you with an unnerving passion, but what drove me mad was that I wanted so much more. I found myself looking besottedly at you as you slept. I wanted to make sure nothing in your life ever hurt you again. I wanted you to be the mother of my children. I knew I was in too deep to ever get out again when I realized that I enjoyed hearing you laugh as much as I enjoyed making love to you."

"And it frightened you," she said quietly.

"It terrified me. Those days in the cottage were idyllic, a dream come true. And then I introduced real life—I asked you to marry me—and like faerie gold the dream crumbled into dead leaves and ashes in my hand. I didn't intend to propose to you, but the words just came because by then I knew I didn't want to live any more of my life without you."

"I really did think having anything to do with me would ruin your life," she said, still unable to believe that the long nightmare was over, that Nicholas was offering her unreserved happiness and joy.

"I know. And you didn't believe I loved you."

"How could I? You hadn't spoken the word, you never even intimated it."

"It meant too much—and I feared to put it to the touch." His mouth curved mirthlessly. "I was shattered and furious that you could believe I'd simply walk out on you, just as bloody St. Clair did. I even wondered whether you were using your parents as a way of keeping me at a distance."

She stared at him, her eyes stormy and bewildered. "What on earth do you mean?"

"Well, it was generally accepted that you left St. Clair flat. He was obviously a mess for months afterward, even rushed into a marriage he clearly didn't want, and I wondered whether you had got sick of him, didn't want to marry him, and then given him the coup de grace by telling him about your parents. I wondered whether history was repeating itself, whether you rejected the men who loved you before they could reject you."

Angrily she tried to pull away. "That would make me sick!"

"It made sense," he countered, scooping her back with effortless ease. "Especially when I tried to persuade you that a generation-old scandal wasn't going to have much effect on my career and you resolutely refused to believe me. It was obvious that you expected me to say, 'Well, it was nice, you were good in bed, but sorry, your parents make it impossible for you to be good enough to be my wife.' It made me too angry to give you the reassurance you needed. I knew then that you would never marry me as long as I was in the diplomatic service. And I wanted to have my cake and eat it, too." His mouth twisted. "Even though I'd been feeling more and more dissatisfied with my life, I needed time to come to terms with the fact that I'd have to give up the service."

She said forlornly, "So it *was* because of me."

"Loving you precipitated a decision I'd have made eventually," he corrected, tilting her chin with his finger so that he could look into her eyes. His were true and direct, holding nothing back. "Your aunt was wrong, Mariel. Of all the people in the world, you deserve to be loved as I'm going to love you."

She nodded, her smile a little wobbly. "I believe you. It never occurred to me that you felt like that."

"I know, darling," he said, the gentleness in his voice infused with a throbbing intensity that convinced her as nothing else could have. "We seem to be dogged by our parents, you and I. You see, I'm more like my mother than I thought. You called me arrogant once. I suspect you were right, but when I organized this reunion I quite coolly decided that if passion was the only way to make you admit that you love me, that we belong together, then I'd use it."

She looked up into blazing green-gold eyes, shivered at the harsh determination in his face, the ruthlessness that lay beneath the civilized surface, and she smiled.

"No," she said lovingly, "you're not like your mother. You'll never be like her. You plotted and planned, yes, but you did it because you wanted me to be happy, not for your own ends."

"Don't canonize me," he said, smiling ruefully. "I'm not so altruistic as all that. I foresee you are going to make me every bit as happy as I intend to make you."

Her mouth trembled. "Oh, I love you," she breathed, touching his cheek. "Somehow you've made me believe that we belong together."

His arms tightened around her with bone cracking swiftness. "About time," he said, laughing beneath his breath.

A LONG TIME LATER she murmured, "What made you go looking for Mr. Svetlanko?"

"After I got over my monumental snit because you'd turned me down—me, the great Nicholas Leigh—I tried to soothe my broken heart by looking into the business. What

I found made me very curious. It was obvious you believed your parents to be guilty."

"I wish I hadn't."

Effortlessly he pulled her down against the hard warmth of his chest. "You were only a kid, and your aunt did a good number on you."

"I should have—"

"*Should have* is what losers say. You only believed what everyone else believed. Stop blaming yourself—you had nothing else to base any beliefs on but what you were told."

"You're so pragmatic," she grumbled, kissing him softly.

He made a quiet noise deep in his chest. "Do you mind?"

She lifted an adoring face to his. "No, never. And you're an idealist, as well. A man who sets up enormous amounts of money for venture capital is almost certainly a closet romantic."

There followed another highly satisfactory interlude, until at last she murmured, "You were telling me about your search for Svetlanko."

"I did some discreet asking around, and the first thing that came to light was the astonishment. Even though people knew of your father's acquaintance with Svetlanko—they were both collectors and friendly rivals—everyone was utterly astounded that your father had turned. And nobody believed that your mother had. It was accepted that your father must have killed her and then himself. I spoke to a couple of people who'd been in Hong Kong then and remembered what had happened, and that reinforced my conclusion that I should look further. Eventually all my leads petered out, except for Svetlanko. I thought that if he was alive he might be persuaded to talk now that the fall of the Berlin wall has changed the world. I contacted him and the rest, as they say, is history."

Nicholas made light of it, but she knew how difficult it must have been for him to find out. The diplomatic service buried its scandals deep.

And then there was the business of finding Svetlanko and persuading him to come to America, the careful planning of the scene . . .

She said with heartfelt intensity, "I don't deserve you."

"That's your aunt speaking." He caught her chin in relentless fingers and turned her face so that he could see her eyes. His were glittering harmonies of gold and green, light and shade, love and the implacable will that no longer frightened her. "You deserve the world in your hands, its joys and laughter running like jewels through your fingers. You deserve everything I can give you, all my love, all my heart, my body and my soul, the children we'll have together. You've spent too long in the shadows, Mariel, too many lonely years. I want to make you so happy you'll never think of them again."

Turning her head, she kissed his upper arm, her mouth soft and tremulous against the coiled power of the muscle.

"I want to make you happy," she said in a choked little murmur. "So happy that nothing will ever hurt you or worry you again. I love you so much, darling, so very much."

"All you need to do to make me the happiest man in the world is be happy yourself," he said. "That's all I want, my darling heart. You with me, forever."

It sounded too much, but she nodded. Oh, there would be unhappiness ahead, she knew that—it was part of the human condition—but as long as they were together they could ride the waves of doubt and uncertainty, sure of their commitment to each other.

The future was no dream born of desire. It was solid, as solid as their love for each other, and it would last.

HARLEQUIN  PRESENTS®

Don't be late for the wedding!

Be sure to make a date in your diary for the happy event—
the latest in our tantalizing new selection of stories...

Wedlocked!

Bonded in matrimony, torn by desire...

Coming next month:

THE ULTIMATE BETRAYAL by Michelle Reid
Harlequin Presents #1799

"...an explosive magic that only (Michelle) Reid can create."
—*Affaire de Coeur*

The perfect marriage...the perfect family? That's what
Rachel Masterton had always believed she and her husband
Daniel shared. Then Rachel was told that Daniel had betrayed
her and she realized that she had to fight to save her marriage.
But she also had to fight to forgive Daniel for this...the
ultimate betrayal.

Available in March wherever Harlequin books are sold.

LOCK10

Harlequin Romance ®

New from Harlequin Romance
a very special six-book series by

MIDNIGHT SONS
DEBBIE MACOMBER

The town of Hard Luck, Alaska, needs women!

The O'Halloran brothers, who run a bush-plane service called Midnight Sons, are heading a campaign to attract women to Hard Luck. *(Location: north of the Arctic Circle. Population: 150—mostly men!)*

"Debbie Macomber's *Midnight Sons* series is a delightful romantic saga. And each book is a powerful, engaging story in its own right. Unforgettable!"
—Linda Lael Miller

TITLE IN THE MIDNIGHT SONS SERIES:

HARLEQUIN PRESENTS®

Harlequin brings you the best books, by the best authors!

ANNE MATHER

"...her own special brand of enchantment."
—*Affaire de Coeur*

&

LINDSAY ARMSTRONG

"...commands the reader's attention."
—*Romantic Times*

Next month:

A WOMAN OF PASSION by Anne Mather
Harlequin Presents #1797

Ice maiden...or sensuous seductress? Only Matthew Aitken
guessed that Helen's cool exterior hid her passionate
nature...*but* wasn't he already involved with Fleur—who just
happened to be Helen's mother!

TRIAL BY MARRIAGE by Lindsay Armstrong
Harlequin Presents #1798

To outsiders Sarah seemed like a typical
spinster schoolteacher.

Cliff Wyatt was the local hunk and could have his pick from a
harem of willing women. So why was he so interested in Sarah?

Harlequin Presents—the best has just gotten better!
Available in March wherever Harlequin books are sold.

BRIDE'S BAY RESORT

UNLOCK THE DOOR TO GREAT ROMANCE AT BRIDE'S BAY RESORT

Join Harlequin's new across-the-lines series, set in an exclusive hotel on an island off the coast of South Carolina.

Seven of your favorite authors will bring you exciting stories about fascinating heroes and heroines discovering love at Bride's Bay Resort.

Look for these fabulous stories coming to a store near you beginning in January 1996.

Harlequin American Romance #613 in January
Matchmaking Baby by Cathy Gillen Thacker

Harlequin Presents #1794 in February
Indiscretions by Robyn Donald

Harlequin Intrigue #362 in March
Love and Lies by Dawn Stewardson

Harlequin Romance #3404 in April
Make Believe Engagement by Day Leclaire

Harlequin Temptation #588 in May
Stranger in the Night by Roseanne Williams

Harlequin Superromance #695 in June
Married to a Stranger by Connie Bennett

Harlequin Historicals #324 in July
Dulcie's Gift by Ruth Langan

Visit Bride's Bay Resort each month wherever
Harlequin books are sold.

HARLEQUIN®

BBAYG

Yo amo novelas con corazón!

Starting this March, Harlequin opens up to a whole new world of readers with two new romance lines in SPANISH!

Harlequin Deseo
- passionate, sensual and exciting stories

Harlequin Bianca
- romances that are fun, fresh and very contemporary

With four titles a month, each line will offer the same wonderfully romantic stories that you've come to love—now available in Spanish.

Look for them at selected retail outlets.

 HARLEQUIN®

SPANT

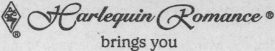
Harlequin Romance ®

brings you

How the West was Wooed!

We've rounded up twelve of our most popular authors, and the result is a whole year of romance, Western style. Every month we'll be bringing you a spirited, independent woman whose heart is about to be lassoed by a rugged, handsome, one-hundred-percent cowboy! Watch for...

• March: CLANTON'S WOMAN—Patricia Knoll

• April: A DANGEROUS MAGIC—Patricia Wilson

• May: THE BADLANDS BRIDE—Rebecca Winters

• June: RUNAWAY WEDDING—Ruth Jean Dale

• July: A RANCH, A RING AND EVERYTHING—Val Daniels